ATTACK OF THE GROWLING EYEBALLS

WHO
SHRUNK
DANIEL
FUNK?
BOOK 1

ATTACK *OF THE*
GROWLING
EYEBALLS

Written by Lin Oliver
Illustrated by Stephen Gilpin

SCHOLASTIC INC.
New York Toronto London Auckland
Sydney Mexico City New Delhi Hong Kong

ISBN-13: 978-0-545-21436-0
ISBN-10: 0-545-21436-X

Text copyright © 2008 by Lin Oliver. Illustrations copyright © 2008 by Stephen Gilpin. All rights reserved. Published by Scholastic Inc., 557 Broadway, New York, NY 10012, by arrangement with Simon & Schuster Books for Young Readers, an imprint of Simon & Schuster Children's Publishing Division. SCHOLASTIC and associated logos are trademarks and/or registered trademarks of Scholastic Inc.

12 11 10 9 8 7 6 5 4 3   10 11 12 13 14/0

Printed in the U.S.A.   40

First Scholastic printing, October 2009

Book design by Lucy Ruth Cummins

The text for this book is set in Minister.

The illustrations for this book are rendered in ink.

For Theo, Oliver, and Cole—my precious sons—L. O.

For Amos—a cool kid who's bigger than he looks—S. G.

ACKNOWLEDGMENTS

Hey, I couldn't have written this book alone. No way. I got help, and I mean big-time. So an in-your-face thanks to Kim Turrisi, my first and best reader. And Ellen Goldsmith-Vein, who kicks butt big-time. And the Simon & Schuster gang, who have awesome taste in publishing. And, of course, to Steve Mooser, who's one funny grown-up, and Alan Baker, who makes my mom laugh, like, 90 percent of the time. And a major shout-out to all my pals in the Society of Children's Book Writers. Hey, dudes, children's book writers rule. No kidding.

—Daniel Funk

THE CAST OF CHARACTERS

DANIEL

PABLO

LARK

VU

GREAT GRANNY NANNY

GOLDIE

ROBIN

MOM

GRANDMA LOLA

PRINCESS

Let's be honest. I have no idea what a prologue is.

And I bet you're not too clear on the concept either.

The only thing I know is that a prologue comes at the beginning of a book. If you ask me, and I know you didn't, I think books should start with a map. You know, a really cool one that shows where the pirate's treasure is buried or where the hobbits live in Middle-earth.

So, I say we blow off the prologue and start this book with a map instead. It's a map of my room, which isn't exactly Middle-earth or anything, and the only treasure that's buried there is an old pair of Batman boxers stuffed under a pile of smelly baseball socks. But it's where I was last Wednesday, the day my story begins. That's the day I shrank down to the size of the fourth toe on my left foot.

Yup, that's what I said. The fourth toe on my left foot.

If you think *you're* surprised, imagine how *I* felt. I went from being a slightly larger than average sixth grader to being the size of a toe. And a pretty small toe at that.

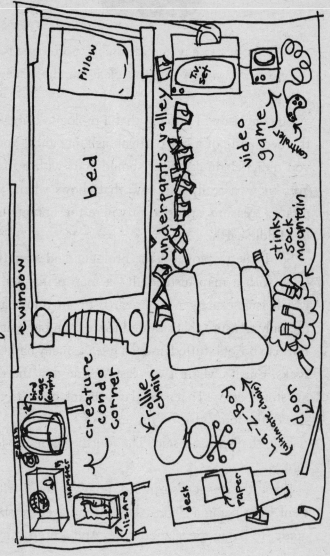

My Room

window

Pillow

bed

underpants valley

TV set

video game

graffaltos

stinky sock mountain

creature condo corner

bird cage (empty)

hamster

lizard

rollie chair

La-Z-boy (ultimate chair)

desk

paper

door

If you're the math-y science-y type and need to know actual numbers, feel free to get out a ruler and measure the fourth toe on your left foot. Go ahead. Knock yourself out. I think you'll find it's about an inch, unless you have really monster feet like I do . . . or are like thirty years old or something. And if you are, then why are you reading this book? It's meant for kids, so close it right now!

Now check out the map of my room and locate the blue leather La-Z-Boy chair. That's my favorite place in the whole world, where I play video games and draw and blow spit bubbles. It's between Underpants Valley and Stinky Sock Mountain. It's also where my story begins.

Visualize me, sitting in my chair last Wednesday when all the weird stuff started happening. And if you're imagining that my room is even the slightest bit clean, don't. I'm here to tell you, it's pretty funky. Now that I think of it, so is my story. But that's how it is when you're Daniel Funk.

Oh, by the way, that's me. Nice to meet you.

CHAPTER 1

The Funkster's Funky Fact #1:
Americans eat 350 slices of pizza per second.

It all started with the pizza.

"Daniel! I'm ordering," my sister Robin said, sticking her head into my room. "What do you want?"

I was sitting in my La-Z-Boy, playing a quick round of predinner video games.

"Triple sausage, double pepperoni, and meatball," I muttered without looking up from the screen.

"Ever heard the word vegetable?" Robin asked, speed dialing Village Pizza on her cell.

"Ever heard the word meat lover?" I answered. I wasn't going to let her lay that "Vegetarians rule" attitude on me.

She came in and flopped herself down on my bed, then shot up really fast when she realized she had flopped herself right onto my sweaty baseball jersey.

"Daniel, you are so gross!" she screamed.

"Hey, can I help it if I have overactive armpits?" I said, firing the word armpit right into her face to really gross her out. She got even, though.

"Hello, Village Pizza?" she said into her hot pink cell phone which I truly believe grows out of her left ear. "This is Robin Funk at 344 Pacific Lane. We'd like a large veggie pizza, hold the cheese. Oh, and extra tomatoes."

Here's a tip: If you have an older sister, never let her order the pizza. You'll wind up getting nothing but salad on a crust. It's a known fact that females order four times more vegetable toppings than guys.

"You left out the meat!" I hollered, lunging for Robin's phone.

But good old Robin, being the star of the eighth-grade volleyball team, has quick reflexes, which meant she escaped into the hall before I could grab her cell. I popped out of the chair and bolted after her, running smack into one of my other sisters, Lark. She was walking down the hall with her Web cam, shooting a boring segment for her boring video blog that no one watches because it's so . . . well . . . boring. Did I mention it was boring?

"Daniel, do you have anything to say to the camera?" Lark turned and focused her egg-shaped mini Web cam on me.

I got real close to the lens and stuck my tongue out. I'm not proud of it, but I confess, I actually licked the lens.

LIN OLIVER

Check that out, bloggy girls!

"Eeuuww, you stink!" my little sister Goldie said as she shoved by me on the way from the bathroom to her room.

"I hope you're planning to take a shower before dinner," Robin chimed in. Wow, this was turning into a "Let's criticize Daniel" session, like always.

"It's stupid to shower before dinner," I answered. "My face will just get all dirty again."

"Most humans eat by putting food *in* their mouths and not *on* their faces," Lark said, moving the camera around so she was shooting her own face talking. I guess she wanted her audience, all two of them, to see her being a ninth-grade know-it-all.

I went back in my room, closed the door, and took

a deep breath. Thank goodness there were no girls there. I live with two teenage sisters, one younger one, one mom, one grandmom, and one great-grandmom. Our dog is female. So is the cat. Even our Siamese fighting fish is a girl.

If you ask me, and I know you didn't, that's a lot of girls in one house. Way too many.

I climbed back into my La-Z-Boy, reclined to the medium position, and burped. Sure, it smelled a little like Granny Nanny's goulash, which I had eaten cold as a postbaseball snack. But I didn't mind. I was glad to be alone in my room where a guy can enjoy his own body odors in peace.

That's when it happened. Bamo-slamo, just like that.

You know how your stomach growls when you're really hungry? That's how it started, except the growling wasn't coming from my stomach. It was coming from behind my eyeballs.

Then my nose felt like it was blowing bubbles.

My fingers started to buzz. My knees whistled.

This was definitely not normal.

"Help!" I screamed.

But my voice wasn't normal either. It was the voice of a small person. A very very very small person.

CHAPTER 2

The Funkster's Funky Fact #2: When you sneeze, air rushes out of your nose at one hundred miles per hour.

I had no idea what was happening to me. I felt like I was disappearing. I checked myself out to see if I was still there.

First I looked down at my hands. Even though my fingers were buzzing like crazy, they looked normal. Five on each hand, with my usual chewed-up fingernails. (I know, I know. I shouldn't bite them, but this is no time to discuss that!)

Then I inspected my knees. They looked regular—well, as regular as knees can look when they're whistling. My left one still had that Z-shaped scar from when I jumped off the skateboard ramp I built in the driveway. (Okay, so maybe it was a little more of a *fall* than a *jump*, but this is no time to discuss that either!) And the other knee had the scab I got after I skinned it sliding into home in the game against the Padres. (By the way, if you ever run into that home-plate ump, tell him I was totally safe and he needs glasses.)

My feet looked normal, too. I brought them up

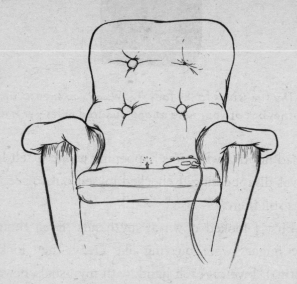

to my nose and gave the toes a sniff. I won't go into details, because I don't want to gross you out so early in this book. Let's just say that my nose told me those were definitely my feet. Enough said.

But when I looked around my room, I realized that everything else had changed. Big time.

All the objects were HUGE.

Like, my TV was gigantic—I mean, as big as a movie screen. The video game controller was the size of the gym at my school. I had to tilt my head way back to see the red and blue action buttons on the top.

I peeked over the edge of my La-Z-Boy. The floor was down there, all right, but *way* down there. I felt like I was sitting at the top of a humongous roller coaster. Last time I was on a roller coaster I barfed up my tuna sandwich, so I decided it would be best not to continue looking down.

I shot a glance over at Stinky Sock Mountain. It was so big, it seemed like Mount Everest, which I had just seen in a National Geographic special in science. I felt like I should climb it and plant a flag in the purple soccer sock at the top.

Creepiest of all was Creature Condo Corner, the table where we keep a lot of our family pets. Cutie-Pie, the Siamese fighting fish, looked like a giant mutant creature from the black lagoon. (I need to mention in a big fat hurry here that I didn't name her Cutie-Pie—my little sister Goldie did.) Lizzie the Lizard (thank you, Goldie, for another totally girly name choice) had teeth as big as a T. rex. And my hamster, Brittany, was the hugest, scariest, hairiest rodent you ever saw. (I know you're thinking it's just like Goldie to name a hamster Brittany, but actually the whole family voted for it. It was six votes for Brittany, one for Rat Face. You guessed it. I was the Rat Face vote.)

What was going on here? Either everything in my room had grown really huge, or I had grown really little. Let's be honest. I was scared.

To calm myself down, I looked into the mirror above my dresser, hoping everything would look normal again. I saw the shelves with all my sports trophies on them. I saw the poster of the red Porsche Carrera on the wall. I saw my blue La-Z-Boy chair.

But I didn't see me!

I stared hard into the mirror. *Where was I?*

Wait a minute! I did see something on the chair. It was a tiny speck of a thing. It was wearing gray baseball pants and a red T-shirt, just like me. It had dark blond floppy hair, just like me. It was staring into the mirror, looking like it had just seen a ghost. And it was about the size of the fourth toe on my left foot.

Holy macaroni, it was me!

A mini me, but me!

I had shriveled up like a raisin, clothes and all.

"Somebody help me!" I screamed.

There were thundering footsteps outside my room, like a giant thumping down the hall. Then I heard my sister Robin.

"Daniel!" Her voice echoed around my room like the announcer at a supersized football game. "Dinnertime."

"Robin! I'm here. In the blue chair!" I called out, yelling so loud I thought my lungs were going to explode.

LIN OLIVER

But she turned and walked away. Oh no, she couldn't hear me! *No wonder,* I thought. *If I'm so tiny, my voice probably is too.*

Here's a tip: When you're the size of a toe, don't count on anyone normal size hearing you.

Suddenly, my nose started to get that bubbly feeling again. I rubbed it hard. Then it began to itch, and I mean itch with a capital *I*. I was going to . . . going to . . . going to . . .

"Ah . . . choooooooooooooooooooooooo!"

I sneezed so hard I thought I might actually blow myself across the room, clear out the window onto Mr. and Mrs. Cole's patio next door.

And then, before anyone could even say "Bless you!" I found myself sitting in my blue chair and back to my normal size.

Just like nothing weird had ever happened.

CHAPTER 3

The Funkster's Funky Fact #3: The nose print of every cat is different, just like the human fingerprint.

I went running out to the living room as fast as my tingling feet could carry me.

"Okay, everyone. Something really strange just happened," I yelled. There was panic in my voice, so I tried to take it down a notch. "Anyone want to guess what?" I asked, trying to sound only mildly weirded out.

"Don't tell me. You took a shower," Robin answered.

She was at the screen door, paying the pizza delivery man. Lark was there too, trying to interview the guy for her blog.

"Do you think the Canadian bacon and pineapple thing is a male-bonding ritual?" she was asking him.

The poor pizza dude looked totally confused. "Hey, I just drop 'em off and collect the money," he stammered. Then he sprinted down our front steps and away from our house as fast as he could. Honestly, can you blame him?

"Would someone like to answer me?" I called out.

I guess not.

Goldie was bringing some paper plates out from the kitchen.

"Hey, Goldfinch," I said to her. "You're not going to believe this, but I just shrunk."

"That's so cool, Daniel. If I shrunk, I'd live in my Barbie dream house and take a Barbie jacuzzi every day."

"This is for real, Goldie. I got really little, and then I got regular again."

"As if you're ever regular," Robin said, as she was passing by to put the pizza box on the dining table.

"Daniel, people don't shrink," Lark said, opening the box and helping herself to a slice. When she took a bite, one of the tomatoes on top actually squirted. If you ask me, and I know you didn't, pizza should never squirt. There's no excuse for it.

"Yeah," Robin chimed in, grabbing an oozy tomato-y slice for herself. "It's all that science-fiction channel junk you watch on TV. It's rotting your brain."

"Oh, not like watching girls volleyball on TV," I fired back at her. "That's good for your brain."

"*Women's* volleyball," Lark interrupted. "Not *girls*."

You can't use the "g" word around my sister Lark. She takes her Woman Stuff pretty seriously. Thank goodness my mom came in and cut off the Woman

Stuff lecture that I could feel was coming. If you're interested in Lark's views, you can read all about them on her website, I'mSoBoring.com.

"Hi, everyone!" my mom called, kicking the kitchen door open. She couldn't use her hands, because they were holding a scraggly gray cat with a patch over one eye. "Say hi to Sam."

"What's wrong with his eye?" I asked.

"*Her* eye," my mom corrected. "Sam is short for Samantha."

"Why do you men assume everything is male?" Lark said. "Samantha is one of *us*, Daniel. She's a *woman*."

"Funny, she looks like a cat to me."

"Sam picked a fight with another alley cat and got a scratch on her cornea," my mom explained. "We're going to keep her for a few days."

My mom's a veterinarian. She has her office in a small house in back of our house, where we live near the beach in Venice, California.

"Mom, please don't tell me Sam is going to be here Friday night," Robin whined.

"She might be. Do you have a problem with that, honey?"

"Major problem," Robin said. "I'm having a party and I don't exactly want a one-eyed alley cat running around creeping out my new friends."

"Why can't Sam come to the party?" my mom asked. "She needs all of our support while she heals."

"No way, Mom!" Robin's voice squeaked like a sick mouse. "This is my pre-pre-pre-pre-prom party!"

"Your prom is four years away, dingbat," I pointed out.

"Well, you can't prepare too soon," Robin said. "I've invited some really cool girls over and we're doing each other's hair and trying on high heels."

"Wow," I muttered. "Who says girls don't know how to have fun."

Robin stuck her tongue out at me. Not to gross you out, but it had some of those slimy tomato seeds on it. Ick. I had to look away.

"What should I wear to the party?" Goldie asked.

"Your pajamas," Robin answered. "Because you'll be in your room, in bed. This is for teenage girls, like Lark and me."

"Teenage *women*," Lark said, just like we all knew she would.

"Lark is trying on high heels?" I laughed. "This I got to see." My sister Lark is definitely the beat-up flip-flop type.

"I'll be there taking notes," Lark said, "for my poetry collection, *Soul Poems for Pre-Prom*."

All right, you guys. Now you see what I'm dealing with here. This is the house I have to live in, where someone can say they're writing a soul poem—wait, not just a soul poem but a *collection* of soul poems—about a prom that isn't even happening for another four years—and no one but me says, *"You've got to be kidding!!!"*

In fact, my mom said, "Why Lark, what an interesting topic."

Interesting? Had her brain turned to chocolate pudding?

"Guys, could we talk about me for a minute?" I said. "Because I happen to have a *real* problem I need to discuss."

Sam the Womanly Cat must not have liked my tone of voice. Either that or she had an attack of temporary insanity. I'm not a cat, so I can't tell you what caused it, but suddenly, she totally freaked out. She sprang out of my mom's arms, eye patch and all, and leaped like a crazed gazelle for the dining table. Bamo-slamo, she landed dead center in the middle of the pizza! I mean, one foot on a tomato, the other on a slice of eggplant.

"Sam!" my mom yelled. "No!"

Sam knew she was in deep trouble, because she shot off the table and raced into the hall, dragging

tomato slime and eggplant skin behind her. My mom
and the girls ran screaming after her.

Whoops, sorry. My mom and the *women* ran
screaming after her.

And there I was, with absolutely zero progress
made on my own situation. We had discussed the
pizza, the party, the soul poems, and the alley
cat. What had never come up was that someone
in our family, namely me, had just had a shrinking
attack.

And that's not the kind of thing you can ignore.

I mean, it's a known fact that shrinking attacks are pretty uncommon. At least, in this dimension of the universe.

I couldn't pretend it hadn't happened. I needed to talk to someone who wouldn't think I had lost my marbles. Flipped my lid. Wigged out.

Lola.

Of course, Lola.

She would understand.

LIN OLIVER

The Funkster's Funky Fact #4: Of all the money spent in the United States to buy toys, 17 percent of it is spent by grandparents.

Lola is my grandmother, my mom's mom. Her real name is Gertrude Gezundheit, but she changed it to Lola. Can you blame her? I bet you'd change your name too if it was Gertrude Gezundheit. Anyway, the reason she picked Lola is because it means grandmother in Tagalog. That's the language they speak in the Philippines.

Oh no, Lola isn't from the Philippines. Nope, nothing that easy for my family. That would be way too logical an explanation.

Lola teaches global culture at my school, which means she knows a whole lot about countries you've never even heard of. Her classroom is decorated with oddball stuff like scary spirit masks from the rain forests of Peru and gnarly camel bags from Egypt and even a slightly smelly stork's nest from Morocco.

A couple years ago, she spent a summer in the Philippines learning how to play the bamboo nose flute.

That's what I said. The bamboo nose flute.

When she came back and moved in with us, she asked all the grandkids to call her Lola. That was cool with me. First of all, I'd do anything for Lola; she's just that great. And second of all, it beats calling her MooMoo, which is what my friend Spencer calls his grandma. MooMoo is a nice lady who makes a fine chocolate-chip cookie, but every time Spence says her name, I see a big spotted cow.

Anyway, back to Lola.

I found her out back in her sweat lodge. Doesn't

your grandma have a sweat lodge in your backyard? No? Then maybe I should explain.

It's a tepee kind of thing but with hot rocks inside. Native Americans heat the rocks in a fire and pour water on them to make steam. My mom freaked out when she discovered Lola was making real fires in our backyard. So now Lola just chucks her sweat lodge rocks in our microwave and nukes them up. She says Grandmother Earth will understand.

"Daniel, come in and purify yourself," Lola said. "You look worried."

I thought I'd get right to the point.

"Lola, I have a shrinking problem."

"You mean, with your clothes in the dryer?"

"No, I mean with my body in the chair. A little while ago, after baseball practice and before the pizza arrived, I shrunk."

If you said that sentence to most people you know, they'd either (a) laugh, (b) send you to a psychiatrist, or (c) have you locked up somewhere far away.

Not Lola. She just poured a little more water on her hot rocks and took a deep breath of the steam.

"The elders teach us that when the world feels too large, sometimes we feel very small," she said.

Lola wasn't laughing at me. But she didn't exactly

believe me either. She handed me a drum and a rattle made from a real rattlesnake.

"Would you like to do some drumming, dear? The Lakota say it will cleanse your mind of negative concerns."

I felt a cool breeze behind me, like someone had opened the flap to the tepee.

Someone had.

"Daniel, come with me immediately." It was Great Granny Nanny, waving me out of the tepee. "And zip your lip."

Great Granny Nanny is in her eighties, but you'd never know it from the way she races around Venice on her mint-green motor scooter, with a matching helmet. Well, sort of matching. The helmet is the same mint green as her motor scooter, but she's painted bright orange flames on it. The flames match the tattoo on her ankle.

Oh, and the one on her wrist, too.

If you ask me, and I know you didn't, all great-grandmothers should be as cool as Great Granny Nanny.

"We've got to talk right now," she said, taking me by the arm and guiding me toward the sunporch at the back of our house where she lives and does her artwork. As we passed my mom's office, I saw through the window that she and Lark and Robin were gathered around Sam the Womanly Cat. I think they were trying to remove eggplant from her toes.

Great Granny Nanny is my dad's grandmother and has lived with us ever since I was born. In fact, she moved in the day after I was born and stayed with us even after my dad died, seven years ago now. He was an ornithologist, which is someone who studies birds. He and my mom were recording the sounds of the rainbow-billed toucan in the South American rain forest when he disappeared. I don't remember him too well, except that he always wore big hats and could whistle like every kind of bird.

By the way, in case you hadn't noticed, my sisters are all named after birds. That's because my mom's a bird nut just like my dad was. I don't even want to tell you my sisters' middle names.

Okay, I will, since you're going through all the trouble of reading this book. They're Lark Sparrow, Robin Flamingo, and Goldfinch Dove. And if you promise not to laugh, I'll even tell you my whole name, just so we can get it out of the way because it's bound to come up sooner or later. Here goes. It's Daniel Eagle Funk. I told you she's a bird nut. All I can say is thank goodness my parents stopped having kids before my mom got to the Yellow-bellied

Sapsucker. I mean, can't you just see me talking to the guys on my baseball team? *Hey dudes, I'd like you to meet my sister Sapsucker.*

"Sit down, hotshot," Granny Nanny said, once we were inside her room. "Believe me, you're going to need to."

I didn't like the sound of that. Not one bit.

CHAPTER 5

The Funkster's Funky Fact #5:
Over the last 150 years, the average height
of human beings has increased by four inches.

There wasn't much room to sit down in Great Granny
Nanny's room. She's an artist. She makes little tiny
sculptures out of little tiny things like buttons and
toothpicks and feathers, and sometimes it's hard to
tell what's a sculpture and what isn't. I didn't want to
crunch any of her art, so I cleared off a space on her
bed just big enough for my rear end.

"I heard you talking to Lola about shrinking," she
began, with a worried look on her face.

"It probably sounds like I've flipped my lid," I said.

"It doesn't sound normal, hotshot. You have to
admit that."

"You know, Granny, I'm starting to think that I just
imagined the whole thing."

"You didn't," she said. "Trust me on that."

There was something in her voice that made my
heart beat faster. I felt like my whole life was about
to change. I had never had that feeling before.

"You didn't happen to have any of my goulash
recently, did you?" she asked.

In case you're not up to speed on your Hungarian great-grandma foods, goulash is like a beef stew with meat and potatoes and carrots and stuff. I think you have to be at least eighty years old to know how to cook it.

"Actually, I ate a whole bowl of goulash when I got back from baseball practice. I was starving."

"Then what?" she asked

"I did a little giccup."

"What's that?"

"A combo gargle, burp, hiccup. Happens sometimes after I eat."

"Then what?"

"Then nothing. I went to my La-Z-Boy, kicked off my cleats, and played video games."

"I wonder," Ganny Nanny said, getting up and starting to pace around her room. "I wonder if the goulash could explain it."

"Explain what?"

"The shrinking."

This was all going really fast for me. I stood up, walked over to Granny Nanny, and looked her right in the eye, which isn't hard to do because she's just my size. This was truth time.

"Granny, are you telling me that I really did shrink?"

"I'm telling you that if you did, you wouldn't be the first in the family."

Whoa. I did need to sit down. I plopped on the bed, and she took a seat next to me.

"There was one before you, Daniel. Back in the old country. Drowned in a bowl of goulash."

"Holy macaroni, Granny. I have a tiny ancestor who drowned in gravy?"

"Goulash gravy. With paprika."

If I said that none of this was making any sense to me, it would be the understatement of the century.

"My grandmother told me of another little one who was taken away," Granny Nanny went on, a faraway look in her eye. "She said they poked and prodded the poor thing until they drove him crazy."

"Who did?"

"Scientists, of course. Couldn't control their curiosity. Finally, he disappeared. Escaped, maybe. Hope so, for his sake."

"Does anyone else know about these . . . these . . . little relatives?" I asked her.

"Just you and me," Granny Nanny answered. "And him."

"Him?"

"I've been waiting to tell you about him," Granny said. "Waiting for the right time."

"Who's him? Him who?"

But before she could answer, the door to her room crashed open and banged against the wall so hard I thought it was going to fly off its hinges. Sam the Womanly Cat, who must have escaped from the eggplant removal session, dashed in and pounced on the bed like a lion. She shot me a nasty look with her one good eye. Maybe she was still cheesed off that I thought she was a guy. Anyway, the next second Sam jumped up on Granny's worktable, stuck her tongue out, and licked up a pile of red sequins. I guess those made her sneeze, which propelled the sequins back out of her mouth at such speed that it sent a shoe box full of feathers high into the air.

"Hey, you, that's art you're messing with!" Granny shouted at Sam.

Sam looked at Granny, then at the floating feathers. She must have thought they were flying mice or something, because she started chasing them like she was the Wild Cat Hunter from Mars. She jumped from the worktable to the wicker chair to the bed, and back to the worktable, finally landing in a basket of Granny's art supplies. Her tail knocked over a cup of paper clips. Her paw sent a bag of glass beads rolling all over the floor. The rattle of the beads scared her, and she leaped into the air, landing on the lace curtains. Her claws ripped the curtains and pulled the rod to the floor, just as my mom and Lark and Robin came running in.

"Sam! No!" my mom screamed.

"Is that all you can say?" Granny Nanny shot back. "That cat is ripping the joint up!"

"Bad cat!" Robin shouted.

Wow, that was creative.

Sam the Womanly Cat continued to run around the room, dragging a fancy tail of lace curtains behind her. Everywhere she went, she knocked something else down.

"I'll get her," Robin said, and lunged for her like she was a loose volleyball on the court. No luck, even for the jock in the family. Sam was fast.

Lark fired up her ever-handy Web cam and started talking.

"This is Lark Funk, reporting from the sunporch. It's human woman versus cat woman here in Venice, as we seek to understand our animal sisters."

Sam yowled and jumped on Lark's back, knocking the camera from her hands. So much for understanding our animal sisters.

Here's a tip: If you're going to learn about your family's shrinking past, do not do it in the same room as a crazed, one-eyed, eggplant-toed cat.

My conversation with Granny Nanny was definitely over. There was not even the slightest possibility of talking, not with all the womanly screaming and shouting and shrieking and cat chasing that was going on there. No way.

To escape the chaos and get a moment to think, I headed back to my room. I have to confess here that my curiosity about the shrinking/goulash connection got the better of me. So on the way to my room, I did make a brief stop at the refrigerator. Just to see if anything would happen.

I opened the fridge, removed the tinfoil from the leftover goulash, and took a swipe at it with my finger. The gravy looked thick and brown and delicious, like the best beef stew you've ever had. But was it magical? Could it make a guy shrink?

I licked the gravy off my finger and let out a giccup

or two. Then I waited. I knew if anything was going to happen, it might take a while.

To pass the time, I checked out the family photos stuck to the front of the fridge. One was of the seven of us at our local beach last Mother's Day, everyone holding a pink rose and blowing a kiss.

Everyone but me, that is. I don't blow kisses. It's one of my rules. I was balancing a Frisbee on my finger and trying to show off the one hair that I've sprouted on my man-chest.

Next to that picture was a shot of our dog, Princess (you laugh, but it's way better than Goldie's first choice of name, which was Miss Flufferball). Her fur was in cornrows that Robin had braided with purple and yellow Lakers-color bows. As if basketball is some kind of fashion show.

The last shot was Halloween last year. All three of my sisters were dressed as fairies. In the middle of them, pretending to eat Goldie's wand, is me, in my bloody mummy wrap. I used two bottles of ketchup to make the blood. It was so crusty and real-looking that our neighbor Mrs. Cole almost threw up when she saw me. Now that was cool.

I stood there looking at the pictures on the fridge for at least two minutes. Nothing happened. That didn't totally surprise me. Great Granny Nanny has a lot of goofball ideas. The idea that goulash could make a guy shrink to the size of a toe was probably just another one of them.

After waiting a respectable amount of time, I gave up. I left the refrigerator and walked down the hall to my room. I decided I had better make a stop in the bathroom for what I thought was going to be a regular pit stop.

But let me tell you this.

It was anything but regular.

CHAPTER 6

The Funkster's Funky Fact #6: The average person visits the toilet about 2,500 times a year. At this rate, you spend three years of your life in the bathroom.

Let's be honest.

You don't want to know the details of what I did in the bathroom. And I don't have a big need to describe it, either. So let's just skip to the flushing part.

As I reached out to flush, suddenly I felt that weird sensation again. The growling noise behind my eyeballs. The blowing-bubbles feeling in my nose. The buzzing in my fingers. The whistling knees.

The last thing I remember hearing was the toilet flush. The rumbling sound got louder and louder and louder. At the end, the roar of the water was so noisy, it sounded like I was smack in the middle of Niagara Falls. I think I passed out for a second. When I opened my eyes, I was surrounded by rushing water, swirling around me in a circle. The current pushed me here and there like I was a tiny twig.

I flipped over on my stomach and tried to swim. The water was deep, but I could see around me. There were no fish or kelp or coral, so I didn't think

I was in the ocean. There was no sand or dirt on the bottom, so it probably wasn't a lake. There was just a white shiny surface all around me and a hole below, like the bottom of a . . .

Toilet!

Holy macaroni! I was swimming in the toilet!

If you ever want to develop a sudden burst of speed with your breaststroke, just try falling in a toilet. You want to get out of there so fast, you'd put a jet engine on your back if you could. I paddled and flopped around like a madman, but the flushing action was still creating current, which made it hard to make any exit progress.

I wondered how big I was. I knew I had shrunk because I had fallen into the toilet. I mean, regular-size people don't fit in toilet bowls. I figured I had gotten very small because the sides of the bowl seemed really far away, so far away that I didn't think I could swim all the way there. But even if I could, I wouldn't be able to get out. Not to be gross, but the inside of a toilet bowl is a pretty slippery surface. It's not like there are footholds or anything.

Luckily, the flushing action stopped. Even though I hadn't gone down the drain, my weak freestyle stroke wasn't getting me anywhere. I wished I could do the butterfly, which is more of a power stroke. At that moment I was so sorry that I'd goofed off doing cannonballs during my summer at Little Dolphins Swim School. I could have used a good butterfly stroke.

All that paddling was making me really out of breath. I mean *seriously* out of breath. I could see the headline now. MYSTERIOUS SHRINKING BOY DROWNS IN OWN TOILET.

While I was gasping for air, I saw something out of the corner of my eye. It looked like a rope, dangling near me. I reached out and grabbed hold of it, but slid right off the end. It was slippery and waxy, like dental floss. I reached for it again, and this time, I noticed it smelled like cinnamon. I put all the clues together. Slippery. Waxy. Cinnamon-scented. Floating in toilet near bathroom counter. There was no doubt about it. It *was* dental floss.

I didn't have time to wonder how it got there, or what was holding it up. I just reached out and grabbed it, and held on tight as I could. When I caught my breath, I started to climb up it. Twice I fell off and landed with a splash back in the toilet. But I knew that this piece of dental floss was my only way out. So I tried again.

I climbed. Hand over hand. Hand over hand. Hand over hand.

Soon, I was above the water line, but still with a long way to go to get to the toilet rim.

Hand over hand. Hand over hand.

I didn't let myself think about falling. I kept telling myself I could make it.

At last the toilet rim came into sight. At least I think it was the toilet rim, because it was white and shiny and smooth. Way beyond it, I could see something pink and gold—like faraway mountains sparkling in the sunset. That could only be one thing . . . our pink plastic toilet seat cover with gold and silver glitter floating inside it. (You guessed it— Goldie picked it out. Robin was hoping for a Lakers one, until I explained to her that NBA players do not become the most elite athletes in the world so they can appear on *toilet* seat covers!)

I wondered if I would be strong enough to actually pull myself up onto the rim of the toilet. During Physical Fitness Week in school, we were required to do five pull-ups. I got close to five; that is, if you count one being close, which I do.

Here's a tip: Do your pull-ups, friends. You never know when you'll shrink to the size of a toe and have to pull yourself onto a toilet rim.

My arms were so tired they were shaking. I wasn't going to be able to hold on much longer. I had to try to get myself out of that toilet, for better or for worse. So I screwed up my courage, let go of the dental floss with one hand and swung myself up toward the rim.

I made it! At least, my left hand did.

Now for my right hand. I let go of the floss, let out a mighty karate shout, and reached for the shiny toilet rim that was looming above my head.

Whoops! I missed. And my other hand wasn't strong enough to support me. I could feel my grip loosening, one finger at a time. I was slipping, no doubt about it!

Just as I was about to plunge back into the water, a hand—the same size as mine—reached out. It grabbed my hand and, with a mighty yank, pulled me up. I think I heard a karate shout, but I was so busy scrambling to reach the toilet rim, I'm not sure what I heard.

Once I was out of the bowl and standing on the slippery white ledge, I looked around to see who had pulled me to safety. When I saw him, I nearly fell back in the toilet.

He was a boy, exactly my size. With dark blond floppy hair, just like me. And freckles on his nose, just like me. And ears that stuck out too much, just like mine.

And here is the weirdest part of all.

He was wearing my face.

CHAPTER 7

The Funkster's Funky Fact #7: Feet sweat about ten to fifteen gallons per foot per year. About five to eight gallons of that perspiration gets absorbed by socks.

When I saw him, I did what any one of you would have done in the same situation.

I passed out.

At least I'm pretty sure I did, because when I woke up, I was back in my room with no memory of how I got there. Actually, I *smelled* where I was before I *saw* where I was. My nose told me I was leaning up against Stinky Sock Mountain. If you ask me, and I know you didn't, it's called stinky for a very good reason.

I picked up my head and looked around. My purple soccer sock was at the top of the pile, and under my body, like a mattress, was a muddy baseball stirrup from my last game. Judging from the hugeness of both socks, I figured I was still in my little-person body.

I had a ton of water sloshing in my ears from my toilet swim. One thing you definitely don't want in your ears is toilet water, even if it is clean. So I stood up and jumped on one leg, to shake the water out.

"Works better if you tap on your head at the same time," a voice said. I looked around and didn't see anyone talking.

"It wasn't easy dragging you here, dude," the voice went on. "I almost busted my gut."

"Who are you?" I asked. "And where are you?"

"Here. Behind the white Nike sock. Sorry to break the bad news, dude, but your feet smell like cauliflower."

"Why are you hiding?" I asked, craning my neck to see if I could get a glimpse of him.

"Uh . . . remember? Last time you saw me, you passed out. I thought this time, maybe we should take things a little slower."

"You're the guy who pulled me out of the toilet?"

"With the help of some handy dandy dental floss," he answered. "Hope you like cinnamon flavor."

"Let me see you," I demanded.

"Sure you're up for it, dude?"

This was crazy. I wasn't going to play games with this guy, whoever he was. I got up and marched right over to my Nike sock. It took all my strength to pull it aside, but I did.

There he was. The boy from the toilet seat. He looked so much like me, it was like looking in a mirror. He held up his palm and flashed me a big grin.

"High-five, dude."

"Who are you?" I asked.

"Pablo."

"Pablo *who*?"

"Pablo Picasso Diego Funk."

"Funk? That's *my* last name."

"Mine too, dude."

Oh, boy. This was spinning into the definite scary

zone. I desperately wanted to shoot back up to my regular size, to go back to the way everything was when I came home from baseball practice. I didn't want to ask any more questions, because I didn't want any more answers. But I think you'll agree that you can't ignore a tiny person hanging out in your dirty-sock pile who looks just like you. I mean, that would be rude, right? So I asked the next question.

"And the reason we have the same last name is because . . . why?"

"We're brothers, dude," he said. "Identical twins. Didn't you notice?"

My ears heard what he was saying but my mind was doing somersaults trying to understand it. I thought I was going to pass out again. I leaned over and put my head between my knees. Unfortunately, that move put my nose closer to the Nike sock. The little dude was right. There was definitely an old cauliflower scent in the air, which didn't help my dizziness one bit.

Pablo moved closer to me and put a hand on my shoulder.

"Hey, bro. I get it. This is a major surprise. We were planning to tell you in a better way."

"We who?"

"Great Granny Nanny. She's been raising me."

"So you're the *him* she was talking about?"

"Beats me, bro. She says a lot of crazy stuff. But she's cool. She teaches me art. You want to see me draw?"

"No," I said. "Are you nuts? This is no time for drawing."

"Hey, it was just an idea," he said. "No biggie."

The shrinking, the brother, the cauliflower feet. It was all hitting me at once, and I needed to think. I may have mentioned that I do my best thinking in my blue La-Z-Boy chair, so I turned away from Pablo and headed for it. It seemed like it was a mile away. I jogged to it, and when I got close enough, looked up at the seat. It was a mile up there, like at the top of a skyscraper. Distances change when you're the size of a toe.

"You want to sit up there?" Pablo asked.

"Yeah, it's my thinking place. You got any ideas?"

"Always, bro. The Pablo is an idea factory."

He looked around, spotted a wide rubber band on the floor, and motioned me over to it.

"Here's the plan," he said, talking to me in an excited voice, like he had just discovered a new planet or something. "I stretch this rubber band out as far as it will go. You stand on it. Then I let go and launch you into the air. You'll fly like a bird, dude. And Bamo-slamo, you'll be in your chair!"

"Bamo-slamo? Hey, I say that."

"Don't I know it, bro. I hear you all the time."

"You do? Exactly how long have you been here?" I asked him.

"Long story, dude. Now do you want to get launched or not?"

"You think it's safe?"

"Sure," he said. "No GUPs around to catch us."

"What's a GUP?"

"It stands for Grown-Up People," he said. "Now are you going or not?"

Actually, it sounded pretty fun. I've always wanted to fly. And since this was already the weirdest day of my entire life, why not go for it totally?

I stepped on the rubber band and bounced up and down a few times. It was springy and wide enough for my feet to balance on it. Pablo slipped the end of the rubber band over his head so it was around his chest.

"Hold on, dude. I'm going long," he called out.

Then he took off running. Past Stinky Stock Mountain. Past my video game controller, which was lying on the floor. Past the leg of the TV stand. Almost to the end of Underpants Valley. The farther he went, the thinner the rubber band underneath my feet became.

"Are you ready, bro?" Pablo hollered when he

couldn't stretch the rubber band any farther.

What was I doing? I was about to be launched across my room, like a circus clown being shot out of a cannon. This was nuts! But before I could call out "NO," Pablo slipped his body out of the rubber band and let it go.

"Blast off!" he shouted.

I was launched! I sailed way up into the air. From the corner of my eye, I could see my whole room under me. My bed, my pets, my TV, my remote control cars. Oh, man, I felt free as a bird. It was great! I got into the tuck position and did a flip, just for grins.

"Nice form, dude!" Pablo shouted. "Way to be!"

By the time I came out of my tuck, I could see the blue chair under me. Oh, yeah! Daniel Eagle Funk, coming in for a landing.

Wait a minute. Now the blue chair wasn't exactly under me. In fact, it wasn't under me at all. It was next to me, in my general area, you could say. But it definitely was not under me.

As I nose-dived down toward the ground, I realized I was going to miss the chair altogether. I was heading for the floor—tumbling downward at about a billion miles an hour.

"Daniel!" a voice called. "Look out!"

I could feel myself falling fast. I saw the hardwood floor coming up to meet me. To make matters worse, I was heading for a landing on my baseball shoe. And it was cleat side up. Trust me, those cleats are sharp. I've gotten a few pokes in my leg when I play catcher.

This landing was going to hurt, big-time.

I closed my eyes, waiting for the crash.

And then I hit.

It wasn't the crash landing I had expected. Actually, it was a soft landing, like I had floated into a squishy, spongy, pink field.

Where was I?

CHAPTER 8

The Funkster's Funky Fact #8: A baby kangaroo, called a joey, is only one inch long when it is born.

"You could have killed yourself, hotshot!"

It was Great Granny Nanny's voice. I recognized that right away.

"It's a good thing I caught you," she said. "You were cruisin' for a bruisin', sonny."

I looked around me. I was in a soft, pink field, all right. And off in the distance I could see orange flames, like the kind Granny Nanny had on her wrist tattoo.

Wait a minute. Could it be? Was I really in the soft pink hand of Granny Nanny? Had she caught me? Was that her tattoo up ahead?

I won't keep you waiting for the answer. It's YES.

She must have come into my room when I was in the air, seen me about to splat on my baseball cleat, and stuck her hand out just in time. Who knew she had such great reflexes? We could use her as shortstop on my baseball team.

I looked up and saw her face staring back at me. It was as big as a giant's.

Granny bent down to the floor and scooped up

Pablo with her other hand. He was still panting pretty hard from his long run across my room.

"And you!" she said to him. "You should know better than to do a crazy thing like that. How many times have I told you not to shoot rubber bands?"

"Three hundred and thirteen," Pablo answered. "But my brain's so little, it doesn't remember much." Then he cracked up. This guy had a mouth and knew how to use it.

Pablo scooted across Granny's palm, ran up her index finger, and when he reached the end, jumped off like he was on a high diving board. He didn't even look where he was going.

"Cannonball!" he shouted, holding his knees to his chest. He sailed across into her other hand, where I was.

"Yo, dude!" He laughed as he somersaulted in next to me. "Was that a fun ride or what?"

"I see you boys have met," Granny said. "Have you told him everything, Pablo?"

"Not everything. He knows about the brother part. But not the whole story."

"What whole story?" I asked. "Could someone please tell me what is going on, right here and now?"

"You deserve to know, hotshot," Granny said. "It's time."

LIN OLIVER

She carried both of us over to my desk and sat down in the broken office chair where I do my homework. She opened her hand flat, and put us down on the desktop. Wow, it was weird seeing my stuff from that angle. My amethyst geode looked like a sparkling purple mountain range. My stapler was like a beast with huge metal jaws. And the extra-strength minty smell from a loose tic tac nearly froze my nose off.

"Where should I begin?" Granny said, pushing her glasses up on her nose. She got down real close to us, so she could see our faces and hear if we said anything. Not to gross you out, but she was so close I could see the hair in her nose. Lucky for me,

Granny Nanny doesn't happen to have a very hairy nose.

"I always wanted to tell you about him, Daniel," Granny began. "But how do you tell a kid that he has a twin brother he's never met?"

"Who's the size of my little toe," I added. "Don't forget that interesting detail."

"Hey, ease off the little toe thing, dude," Pablo said. "I am way bigger than your little toe."

"Okay, so you're the size of my fourth toe. What's the difference?"

"Hey, when you're my size, every little bit matters."

"I am your size," I reminded him.

"I don't know if you'll stay that way," Granny said. "We really don't know much about the shrinking gene in our family—who gets it, how it works, when it kicks in. It's all a mystery."

"Did my dad shrink?" I asked.

"Never knew him to," Granny said. "And I certainly would have known."

"What about you?"

"Nope, I never did. Neither did my father. So I thought we were done with it."

"And that's why you never told anyone?"

She nodded. Then she sighed, like she was preparing to say something that was difficult for her. When she exhaled, the force of her breath totally knocked me over. I had to grab on to my stapler to keep from blowing off the desk entirely.

"Now Daniel, this is going to be the hardest part for you to understand," Granny said. "Pablo was born at the same time you were. No one saw him at first, because he was tiny even then."

"So, like, when I was born, he was in my hand or something?" I asked.

"Actually, I was in your ear, dude. Curled up like a baby kangaroo."

Okay, this was now officially too weird for me. Just the thought of Pablo . . . of Pablo . . . well, imagine you had a twin brother who came into the world curled up in your ear like a baby kangaroo. If you can wrap your head around that, I think you'll know how I was feeling at that moment. Yeah, like I was watching myself on the sci-fi channel.

"I think I'll be going now," I said. "I have math homework, and it really can't wait."

I reached for one of the yellow pencils on my desk. Math homework never sounded so good.

Here's a tip: Don't try lifting a pencil when you're less than an inch tall. You'll just break out in a sweat and drop it on your foot.

"Trust me, hotshot. You'll get used to the idea,"

Granny said, lifting the humongous No. 2 soft lead off my foot.

"Having a baby brother born in my ear?" I said. "No, that's not the kind of idea a guy gets used to."

"He was so precious," Granny said with a little smile on her wrinkly face. "I noticed him when I came to the hospital to give you your first bath."

"So you saw him and you didn't scream, '*Somebody help . . . there's a mini baby in this kid's ear?*'"

"Oh, no. I knew I couldn't tell anyone about him. Not anyone."

"Not even Mom?"

"Not even her. Maybe that was a mistake, but all I could think about was what had happened to that poor little fellow back in the old country. Poked and prodded by scientists until they drove him crazy. With no one there to protect him."

"So you moved in with us to protect him?"

"The very next day," she said. "And he's lived here, with us, ever since."

"Here? Where?"

"She makes really cool houses for me," Pablo said. "Lately, she's been letting me go on sleepovers. Last week, I slept in the turret of your Lego castle. Those plastic guys at the door are real stiffs, dude."

Then he cracked up. Actually, I did too.

"And swear you won't tell this to the sisters," he went on, "but I've been known to hang out in their Barbie dream house. The jacuzzi's awesome."

I considered how Goldie would react if she knew he'd been soaking in her Barbie jacuzzi. I bet she'd kind of like it. She was only nine and hadn't been totally ruined by Lark and Robin yet.

"Recently, I've tried to talk to your mother about Pablo," Granny Nanny said. "But she thinks I'm bonkers."

So that was it. I remembered overhearing a conversation between my mom and Lola a couple of weeks before. It was Chinese New Year and Lola was in the kitchen, whipping up a batch of fish balls and lotus roots for a feast. I heard my mom telling her that sometimes Granny talked about little people and that maybe she was starting to imagine things, like some older people do. After that, Mom tried to get Granny to see a doctor, but she refused.

My head was spinning. Pablo had checked out of the conversation. He had gotten involved in trying to balance on one of my pencils as it rolled along the desk. He was biting his lower lip in concentration, just like I do when I'm up at bat.

It's weird to look into your own face. His hair was messier than mine. His face was dirtier. And his clothes were different. He was wearing floppy boots and rolled-up army pants that looked like they'd been made from the costume of one of my old action figures. And I could tell his red cape was definitely a cut-up Superman cape, even though someone had sewn a tiny yellow *P* on it. Could he really be my twin? I decided to give him a pop quiz.

"So, when's your birthday?" I asked.

"February second, Groundhog Day. Just like you, dude."

"And your dream car is . . ."

"Porsche Carrera. Red. Just like you, dude."

"And your favorite food?"

"Spaghetti, just like you, bro. Except that one noodle lasts me a whole week."

"Anything weird about your body? Aside from the fact that you're . . . well . . . should I say . . . on the short side?"

"Got three freckles on my back, in the shape of a triangle," he said, pulling up his T-shirt to show me.

I picked up my shirt to show him the three freckles on my back that exactly matched his. And that's when it happened. My nose started to itch with a capital *I*. Then came the sneeze to end all sneezes.

"Ah . . . ah . . . ah . . . ah . . . ahchoooooooooo!"

And before you could say Pablo Picasso Diego

Funk, I shot up to my regular size. It took maybe a second.

And wouldn't you know it, that was the very second that Robin Flamingo Funk chose to come into my room. She just stared at me, standing on top of my desk, my head almost touching the ceiling. I could tell she couldn't see Pablo, which wasn't that strange. I mean, he had been around for eleven years, and I had never noticed him either.

"Okay, brainless," Robin said. "What do you think you're doing?"

"Hey, can't a guy stand on his desk when he feels like it?"

"Granny, how can you let him act so weird?" she said. "It's so annoying—not to mention embarrassing."

"We're doing an art experiment," Granny Nanny said. "Daniel is standing on his desk to see what it would be like to draw the world through the eyes of a tall person."

Holy macaroni. She was good. I mean, she didn't blink an eye. She just opened her mouth and let that whopper story rip.

"Daniel, since I'm having a party here on Friday," Robin said, "with some very normal people, I'd appreciate it if you could try to act at least slightly normal for a few hours. If that's not too much to ask."

"No problem, Robs," I answered. "Normal is my middle name."

I did a little rump wiggle on top of the desk, just to show her how not true that was.

"Honestly, this family," Robin said. "A one-eyed alley cat. A rock-nuking grandma. And now, a desk-walking, rump-twitching brother. How weird can it get?"

I squinted down at my desktop. There was Pablo in his army boots, jumping up and down on my pink eraser like it was a trampoline.

And I thought: That's how weird it can get.

CHAPTER 9

I had to get to the bottom of this shrinking thing. I mean, was this just a freak thing that happened because I had eaten Granny's goulash on the last Wednesday in February? Or was it going to be a regular part of my life that could happen at any time? Was I going to become permanently tiny? Let's be honest. Shrinking to the size of your fourth toe on your left foot is fun once or twice, but I think you'll agree that being a full-time shrinking person has its problems.

Granny and I decided that I would stay home from school the next day. We'd tell my mom that I wasn't feeling well. Then when she was out in her office, we could experiment with the goulash and see if we could figure out exactly what made me shrink and unshrink.

After we'd made the next day's plans, Granny scooped Pablo up into her hand and started back to her room. As they left he said something, but I couldn't hear what it was. It was almost impossible to hear him when he was small and I was big.

I ran out into the hall and caught up with them.

"What'd you say?" I whispered to Pablo, sticking my nose into Granny's hand.

"I said later, gator."

"Well then . . . hasta, pasta," I whispered back.

I put out my pinkie finger and he gave it a teensy high five. It felt like a butterfly wing brushing up against my hand. I liked it.

When I looked up, there was Lark staring at me from the bathroom where she was flossing her teeth.

"Why are you talking to Granny's hand?" she asked.

"Because I believe we need to communicate with our fingers. They live a lonely life way out at the end of our hands."

Any normal person would have told me I was crazy and kicked the bathroom door shut. Not Lark.

"Never thought of it that way," she said. "Mind if I blog about it? When I'm finished writing my feelings about flossing, that is."

"Only if you promise to tell everyone that cinnamon dental floss saved my life," I said.

Sometimes when you tell the truth, it's the last thing people want to hear. This time Lark just shook her head and kicked the door closed.

It wasn't until I was alone in my bed that night that the truth hit me with full force. Not the truth about me being a shrinking guy. No, that wasn't what was rolling around and around in my head. Another thought was. And it was this.

I have a brother. An actual brother.

I had always wanted a brother. And now I had one.

Yes, he was little.

And yes, I hardly knew him.

And yes, he was a secret.

But he was my brother. Not a sister or a mom or a grandmom or a great-grandmom. But a guy, like me. My other half.

Don't get me wrong here. I like girls. (Excuse me, Lark. I like *women*.) I even love some, like my sisters and my family. Oh, I don't love them all the time, but I have been known to love them occasionally. But, and this is a big but, I would be lying to you if I said that anything they do makes even a little bit of sense to me. We're just different, that's all. And they don't get that. So they spend their lives trying to change me, which is why "Let's criticize Daniel" is the favorite sport in my house.

Like, I'll be at the table eating dinner, and nine times out of ten, one of them will tell me to use a napkin to wipe my mouth. Why not just use your shirt, since at some point you're going to wash it anyway? And for that matter, why wipe your mouth after every bite? I mean, you're just going to slobber it all up again. Why not just let all the food pile up there until you're done, and give it one humongous wipe after the meal?

Or if I'm sitting in the living room watching TV and I let out even a little burp, what do they say? *Daniel, cover your mouth when you burp.* Why? I mean, if you cover your mouth, you're just going to wind up breathing in your own gas, and that can't be good for your lungs.

There are so many questions that come up when you're living in a house of all women. Like why they cry when they're happy, or comb their hair when it's not messed up, or dance with the doorknob, or talk during football games when it isn't even halftime.

I'm just telling you this so you can understand that for me, having a brother who wasn't going to ask me why I had to leave my shoes in the middle of the living room or say "Eeuuww, you're so gross" after every single thing I did, was . . . well . . . it was too cool for words.

When I realized that, I knew I had to take action. I got out of bed and went straight into Granny Nanny's room.

"I want him to move in with me," I said to her. "In my room."

"That's so nice, hotshot, but it's not safe for him there," she said. "My room is Pablo-proofed."

"So we'll Pablo-proof mine. He's my brother. I want to grow up with him."

"Ease up, bro," Pablo said, popping out of one of Granny's artworks that was perched on the windowsill. "If you hadn't noticed, growing up is not exactly my specialty."

I had to get real close to him and listen hard to hear what he was saying. That gave me a chance to check out Granny's little sculpture close up. Now that I looked carefully at it, I realized it was a tree house made from twigs and feathers and pine needles. In fact, as I looked at them scattered around her room, I realized that all of Granny's sculptures were houses for Pablo—a castle made from clay, an Eskimo-type igloo made from blue glass beads, even a tepee built with scraps of old leather shoes. So that's why everything she made was so small.

"Tell you what," Granny said. "He can sleep in your room tonight. After all, it's a special occasion. Live it up, that's what I always say."

I threw my arms around her and gave her a hug.

"You're quite a woman, Granny," I said.

"Girl," she answered.

"Which house should we take?" Pablo asked me. He was already gathering a few little clothes together.

"How about the igloo," I said. "It's really cool." And then I laughed, because it's a known fact that if there's one thing an igloo is, it's cool.

Pablo climbed inside it, and I left Granny's room, carrying the beaded blue igloo down the hall. I passed

LIN OLIVER

Lark's room. She was typing on her computer, so I popped in. I admit, it was pretty fun to know that I was holding her minibrother, and Miss Know-It-All didn't have a clue.

"How's the blog?" I asked. She looked surprised. It was the first time I had ever said those words, or anything like them.

"Well, I'm finishing my flossing piece," she said. "It's called 'Can Dental Hygiene Bring You True Happiness?'"

"Wow, I can't wait to read it," I said.

"Liar," said a little voice from inside the igloo.

I cracked up. Lark looked really pleased.

"I'm glad you like it, Daniel," she said. "At last you're maturing."

As I left and headed back down the hall, I tapped on the top of the igloo.

"Hey in there. You got to quit cracking me up like that."

"I can say anything I want," Pablo said. "My voice doesn't carry very far, so the only one close enough to hear me is you."

"Yeah, but it looks like I'm laughing at nothing," I explained. "Which normal people don't do."

"Who wants to be normal?" Pablo said. "Where's the fun in that?"

When I stuck my head in Robin's room, she was on the phone, no surprise there.

"We're meeting here Friday at seven for veggie burgers and salad," she was saying to one of her pre-pre-pre-pre-prom pals.

"Barf food," Pablo said from inside the igloo. I cracked up again. Robin flashed me her get-out-of-here look, and I did.

Only Goldie suspected that something was different.

"Where are you taking Granny's artwork?" she said, when I peeked in her room, which used to be a big closet but had been redone so there was just enough room for a bed and her toys.

"Hey, I like art as much as the next guy."

"Art rhymes with fart," I heard Pablo say from inside. That did it. I totally lost it. I started to laugh so hard that I actually got a pain in my side. If you ask me, and I know you didn't, that was the funniest thing anyone had ever said.

"Could you leave now?" Goldie said. "You're creeping me out."

I went howling out of her room and into my own. I put Pablo's igloo on the table next to my bed and flopped down on my race-car bed, still laughing like a hyena.

After I recovered I got my flashlight and shined it inside the igloo, to make sure Pablo was safe and hadn't gotten shaken around too much by the trip down the hall. I could see him but not that well. So I got a magnifying glass from my desk drawer and propped it up against the igloo door.

Now when I looked in, Pablo appeared to be ten times bigger. He was taking off his army pants and putting on some sweats. I could see that they were made from an old baseball jersey of mine when I was on the Astros.

"Hey, bro. A little privacy here. I'm changing."

"I just wanted to say good night," I said. "Sorry if I bothered you."

"No biggie," he said.

"And Pablo," I whispered. "I'm really glad you're here."

"Likewise, dude," he answered.

I flicked off the flashlight and took down the magnifying glass. As I settled back on my pillow, I smiled to myself. Here we were. Just me and my bro, kicking back for the night.

I fell asleep smiling.

CHAPTER 10

The Funkster's Funky Fact #10:
Humans are the only animals that sleep on their backs.

"Mom, I'm not feeling so good," I said the next morning as I dragged into the kitchen, trying to sound sick. The whole family, including Sam the Womanly Cat, was sitting around our breakfast nook. Granny Nanny was already at the stove, warming up some of the leftover goulash in her favorite iron pot.

"I'm so sorry, honey," my mom said in her vet voice, which is very soft and gentle. "Where does it hurt?"

"Eyes, throat, nose, knees. The usual."

"He's faking it," Robin said.

"I am not," I snarled back at her. "Here, look at my throat. It's got green stuff in it."

I went over to our turquoise leather breakfast booth where she was sitting, got up real close to her, and opened my mouth in her face. I knew she wouldn't look.

"Eeuuww, Daniel, get away from me!" Robin shrieked. "Like I care about your mucous."

"I'll make you some billy goat weed tea, dear," Lola

offered. "The natives of Suriname use it to cure sore throats."

"I'll be okay, Lola," I said quickly. You never want to drink her tea. She brews up all kinds of herbs and bark and stuff, and it always tastes like you swallowed a tree. "I just need to drink some orange juice and sleep."

"Daniel, I can't stay home with you today," my mom said. "I'm delivering a lecture at the university on feather loss in the peach-faced lovebird."

I didn't even flinch. Stuff like that comes out of my mom's mouth all the time. One minute she's talking about whether we should have brownies or coconut cake for dessert, the next minute she's yammering on about the causes of swollen beak disease in the Australian cockatiel.

"I can watch him," Granny Nanny said. "I was planning to hang around and paint some new flames on my motor scooter. I'll fire up the TV for him. We'll be fine."

My mom glanced over at Lola. I could tell she wasn't completely comfortable with leaving me alone with Granny Nanny. Last time she watched me, I talked her into taking me for a ride on the back of her scooter, and my mom had a fit.

"I'll call every couple hours to see that everything's

okay," Lola said. "School is only five minutes away."

The doorbell rang.

"That's probably Vu," I said. "I've got to tell him that I'm not going to school today."

Vu Tran lives in the green-and-white house two doors down from our big red bungalow on Pacific Lane, and most mornings we walk to school together. I guess you could call him my best friend, even though we don't hang out together that much. His parents are from Vietnam, and they own a little restaurant near the beach. He goes there after school so they can supervise his homework. He doesn't mind, though, because he's not a big fan of hanging out in our house anyway. He's allergic to dog hair, plus Goldie has a crush on him and is always asking him to play Monopoly with her. If those two things aren't annoying enough, my older sisters give him a hard time about his hair, which he spikes up with a ton of gel.

"Hey, man," I said to Vu when I opened the screen door. "I'm not going today."

"Are you sick or is it a mental health day?" he asked.

What do you say? I mean, I didn't want to lie to my best friend. But I couldn't exactly tell him I was taking the day off to hang out with my new miniature brother.

LIN OLIVER

"I'm kind of sick," I lied.

"Too bad," he said. "Ms. Waters is bringing in her pet hissing cockroach for us to observe."

This is the kind of thing that excites Vu. Hair gel and science are his two big interests.

"Sorry to miss it, man," I said, which I sort of was. I'd never met a hissing cockroach before. "I should be better tomorrow."

"I'll ask her if the cockroach can stay until then," he said as he banged the screen door in my face and hurried down our wooden steps.

I closed the door fast. I had important stuff to get to and limited time. Even though Robin was staying late for volleyball practice, and Goldie had Chemistry Club, and Lark had a meeting of her Poetry Society (she's president, naturally), my mom was going to be home by three. I had a lot of questions that had to get answered before then.

By eight thirty everyone had finally cleared out. Granny Nanny took Sam into the back office, so she wouldn't freak out again. We put Princess in Robin's room with a big chew stick to keep her busy. Granny went into the kitchen to check on the goulash, and I went into my bedroom to get Pablo.

I stuck my finger in the door of the igloo and waved it around in there.

LIN OLIVER

"Dude, I'm sleeping here," he called out. "What time is it anyway?"

"Almost nine o'clock," I told him.

"In the morning? Are you crazy? The Pablo doesn't get up until noon. I need my rest, bro."

I hadn't really thought about what his life was like. Why would he get up early? He had no school. No chores. No baseball or soccer practice. Nothing to do but have fun.

Pablo was clearly not interested in getting up on his own. He was going to need some encouragement. So I got the magnifying glass and leaned it up against the igloo door. When I looked through it, I saw Pablo inside, sprawled on his back in a little bed that was made from a seashell filled with cotton balls. He was out cold.

I blew into the igloo door and when my breath hit his face, he sat up.

"Whoa, who's got the toothpaste breath?" he said. "It's burning my nose hair."

Man, he looked a mess. His hair was standing straight up like Vu's but with no hair gel added. He rubbed his eyes and squinted out the door at my eyeball peering in on him.

"Morning, Pablo," I said. "The coast is clear. No one's here but me and Granny. Let's go in the kitchen."

"You got food?" he said.

"I can arrange that," I answered.

"Food is good. I'm starving."

He rolled out of his bed, stepped around the magnifying glass, and hopped into my hand. He stretched and yawned like a mini bear waking up from a winter's hibernation as I carried him into the kitchen.

While Granny dished up some goulash for me, Pablo ate a cornflake.

You heard me. Not a *bowl* of cornflakes. *One* cornflake.

In the meantime I sat down and ate the whole bowl of goulash.

"I have a stopwatch here," Granny Nanny said when I finished it. "I want to see how long it takes for you to shrink. We need to get scientific about this."

She clicked the stopwatch and we waited. Two minutes. Five minutes. Ten minutes. Pablo was lying on the table, holding his stomach and moaning and groaning about how full he was from his one cornflake binge. I got up and did twenty-five jumping jacks. I thought maybe exercise would hurry things up. When I was doing the jumping jacks, I noticed I couldn't hear Pablo. But I could tell he was moaning from the way he clutched his stomach and rolled around.

"Now do you feel anything?" Granny asked me when I had finished and sat back down at the table.

"Nope," I said.

We waited some more. I drummed my fingers on the table and stared at all the stuff we kept there. The salt and pepper shakers. A sugar bowl. A glass jar with big green straws in it. Both Goldie and I like to drink chocolate milk with those fun fat straws.

Suddenly I had an idea. If you ask me, and I know you didn't, I thought I had come up with a fantastic invention. Not quite as good as the telephone, but definitely up there. I reached into the jar and pulled out five straws. Very carefully, I fit one straw into the other, so that they made a connecting straw tube, about four feet long. I handed one end to Pablo, then put the other end to my ear.

"Talk," I said to him.

"Pablo to mission control," he said into his end of the straw. "Do you read me?"

Oh yeah, I read him loud and clear. His voice shot through the tube and landed right in my ear hole, like he was standing right next to me.

"It works!" I shouted. "My invention works."

"Bro, could you keep your voice down?" Pablo said into the straw. "The volume's pretty cranked up down here."

"This must be how Alexander Graham Bell felt when he invented the telephone," I told Granny. "I'm going to call this the PabloPhone."

"Like the name, dude," Pablo said into his end of the straw. "Very classy."

"We'll use this whenever I'm big," I said to him.

"Which is looking like it may be most of the time, hotshot," Granny said. "It's been twenty minutes, and you haven't shrunk an inch."

I considered the possibility that I might never shrink again. I wouldn't miss the growling eyeballs and whistling knees part. But I would definitely miss being able to hang out with Pablo, to look him square in the eye, to hear every word he said.

"Is the goulash any different today than it was yesterday?" I asked Granny.

She thought about that a minute. "Well, Robin did pick out all the carrots last night. She put them on her leftover pizza."

"Carrot pizza," Pablo said into the tube. "Yuck, I'm going to hurl."

At last, another meat lover in the family.

"It's got to be the carrots then," I said, thinking out loud. "If they're the only thing missing, then it has to be the carrots that make me shrink."

"Let's test that," Granny said. "I'll add some

carrots to the goulash right now, and we'll see what happens."

This was science at work.

Granny looked in the refrigerator. We had celery and lettuce and tomatoes, but not a carrot to be found.

"I'll go to the market," she said. "You have to wait here. I'm under specific directions from your mother

never to take you on the scooter again. Can I trust you not to get into any trouble?"

"Trouble?" I said. "Never heard the word."

"I have," Pablo said into the PabloPhone. Fortunately, Granny couldn't hear him.

"I'm trusting you, Daniel," she said, putting on her helmet with the flames and grabbing her keys. "Stay right here at the kitchen table. Don't move. And that goes for you too, Pablo."

"No problemo," he said into the straw. "The Pablo is digesting."

"Me too," I said, letting loose a little giccup just to emphasize the point.

Granny opened the back door and headed out to the garage. I heard her scooter engine rev up, then start to putt like it does when she backs out of the garage. Then it switched to its regular drone as she took off down the back alley.

I stayed still. I didn't move a muscle. At least, I didn't mean to.

But here's a tip: When your eyeballs start growling and your nose starts bubbling and your fingers start buzzing and your knees start whistling, it's really hard to stay still, even if you promised to.

CHAPTER 11

The Funkster's Funky Fact #11: Looking at a bright light will cause one in four people to sneeze. It's called the photic sneeze reflex, and it's for real!

Bamo-slamo!

Within two seconds after Granny left I had shriveled up like a raisin, clothes and all.

Somehow I managed to hang on to the breakfast table when the shrinking sensations began. So instead of falling off the chair onto the ground, I found myself suspended from the table by one hand. It was pull-up time again, just like the day before in the toilet.

I pulled myself up with all my might, letting out a karate holler like they do in martial arts movies. It worked, and as I crawled onto the table, I found myself looking eye to eye with Pablo.

"Welcome to my world, dude," he said. "I guess it's not the carrots."

"I don't get it," I said, pacing back and forth on the breakfast table. "I ate more goulash just now than I did last night, but it took me longer to shrink. You'd think the more I ate, the faster I'd shrink."

"Yeah, it's a mystery," Pablo said. "Want to play?"

"Granny said not to move."

"Right. But she didn't say not to slide."

He grabbed the PabloPhone and angled it straight down to the floor.

"Now all I need is something to make it slippery," he said with a grin. "Aha!"

He took a few mouthfuls of Robin's leftover cereal milk and spit the milk into the straw.

"Sure, you got your water slides," he said. "Now check out Pablo's Monster Milk Slide."

With that he dove headfirst into the straw. I could hear him whooping it up from inside the tube as he slid all the way down to the kitchen floor. When he crawled out the other end, he was soaked in milk and laughing like a wild man.

"Yo, dude," he shouted into the straw, which had instantly become the PabloPhone again. "You got to try this. It's awesome."

Should I or shouldn't I? Granny said not to move. But a milk slide? Come on, it was just too cool to resist. Admit it, guys. You'd do the same thing.

And it was the right decision. The ride was double awesome. I went whishing down that straw on my stomach at a gazillion miles at hour. I had to keep myself tucked pretty tight, because there wasn't a lot of room inside there. But that actually made the ride faster. I just whizzed straight down, going so fast I could hardly catch my breath.

Pablo was waiting for me at the other end.

"What should we do next?"

"Granny Nanny should be back any—"

"Let's go for a swim," he interrupted. Man, this guy was all fun, all the time.

"Okay, but no toilets," I said. "Been there, thanks."

He dragged me over to the laundry room just off the kitchen.

"There's our pool," he said, pointing to Princess's water dish. "I take a dip here most days."

"You swim in a dog bowl?" I said.

"Mom changes the water every morning just before she goes out to the office," he said. "And Princess doesn't touch it until noon. I know the routine by heart."

Pablo pulled a dog biscuit out of the box we keep next to the washing machine. He dragged it over to the dish, so he could use it as a step to climb up the side. It wasn't quite high enough, so I went to get another biscuit. As I stuck my head in the box, I thought I heard the phone ring. There was no way I could get it. It was twenty times as big as I was.

We piled the second dog biscuit on top of the first

one to make stairs up to the bowl. Pablo pulled off his shirt, climbed up and stood on the ledge of the doggy dish.

"Jackknife!" he called out, and did a perfect dive into the dog bowl, touching his toes before he hit the water. He didn't even make a splash.

"Now you go!" he shouted to me, after he came up and swam to the side.

I don't know how to do a jackknife dive, but I can do a backflip. So I pulled off my shirt, climbed up to the edge of Princess's dish, stood backward with my heels hanging off the edge, and flipped into the water.

"Great one, bro!" Pablo yelled. "A perfect ten!"

We went through every dive I ever learned, then made up a few silly ones of our own.

"Swan dive while sticking your tongue out," Pablo called.

"Pigeon-toed cannonball!" I yelled.

"Belly flop while oinking like a pig!" Pablo said, oinking.

"Racing dive with a zombie walk first!" Pablo had never seen a zombie movie, so I had to teach him how do to a zombie walk. He caught on real quick.

"What now?" Pablo asked, as we were drying off and putting our shirts back on. He looked around the laundry room. "I know. Skiing."

This I had to see. Where was he going to get snow in Venice, California?

"Here's the deal," he said, putting his hand on my shoulder. "We spill some of that detergent onto the floor and make a powder mountain. Then we ski down."

"Where do you get these ideas?" I asked him.

"I told you, bro. The Pablo is an idea factory."

Man, this beat school any day.

We went to the detergent box and tried to push it over. It was heavy.

"We're going to have to do better," Pablo said. "Lean on it and push with your shoulder. Count to three and GO!"

"One. Two. Three." I pushed and grunted with all my might. Bamo-slamo, the box of detergent fell over. White laundry powder poured out and built up into the shape of a perfect ski mountain.

"Now we need skis," Pablo said, looking around the laundry room. We hunted through lots of stuff on the floor—balls of lint, an old sponge, a couple of black markers. There was nothing we could make into skis. I might have given up, but not Pablo.

"Plan B," he said.

He took me over to a roll of plastic garbage bags

my mom stores on a low shelf with all the other supplies. Each bag had a red plastic tie at the top that you pull to close up the bag. Pablo grabbed one of the ties.

"Help me tear off two pieces of this," he said. It wasn't hard because the plastic was really thin.

"Now what?" I said. I still wasn't on board with Plan B.

He didn't answer, just motioned me to follow him. We went over to the detergent mountain. Pablo looked it up and down.

"The powder's fresh," he grinned. "Let's attack."

He let out a whoop and started up the mountain. I followed. As we climbed, we left footprints in the snowy white powder, just like real explorers do. When we reached the top, Pablo put the red plastic down on the mountain and lay down on top of it like it was a sled.

"Wish me luck," he said, and pushed off with his hands. The mountain was steep and he rode his homemade sled down pretty fast. When he reached the bottom, he kept going, not coming to a stop until he was halfway across the slippery linoleum floor.

"Smooth ride!" he hollered. "Next time we'll add some water for speed."

I jumped on my red plastic sled and pushed off

too. As I crisscrossed the mountain, I looked to the right. Under the washing machine, tucked way back, was my other purple soccer sock. That sucker had been missing in action for months. It's amazing what you see when you're little.

When I reached the bottom, I was expecting a high five from Pablo. But he was standing very still and quiet, his hand cupped to his ear.

"I hear a GUP. I know their footsteps."

"It's Granny Nanny," I said.

Pablo shook his head. "No scooter sound," he said. "And this one's coming in the front way. Granny comes in the back."

We crept across the laundry room into the kitchen. From there, we could see all the way across the living room to the door.

There was definitely someone on the front porch. And that someone was definitely putting a key in the front lock. The door opened.

It was Lola.

"Daniel!" she called out. "I phoned and no one answered. Are you okay?"

Oh boy. Things had suddenly gotten very complicated. I mean, I couldn't say, "Sure Lola, I'm fine, I just happen to be the size of a toe right now."

"What should we do?" I asked Pablo.

"I don't know, dude. I was thinking about taking a jacuzzi."

"I can't do that. Lola's looking for me. She'll panic if I'm not here and call mom and then they'll all be looking for me."

"Pays to be small, dude," Pablo said. "No GUPs looking for me. No one on my tail. No worries."

"Daniel!" Lola called again. She had gone in my room and come out. "Answer me right now!"

In the back of the house I heard the *putt putt putt* of Granny's engine, pulling into the garage.

"Saved by the scooter," Pablo said.

Even though Granny was coming back, I didn't feel saved. In fact, she was only going to make matters worse. Now Lola would ask her where I was, and what was she supposed to say? If she said she let me go outside and didn't know where I was, they'd never let her watch me again. And if she said I had shrunk, they'd think she was bonkers. The last thing I wanted to do was get Granny into trouble, too.

I needed to unshrink. Right then and there. That was the only way out of this.

But how to do that? What made me unshrink before?

Right, I know what you're thinking—sneezing. And I should have thought of that too. But understand, guys, I was in a clutch situation and I confess, I was choking a little. The old brain just wasn't kicking into gear.

As Lola walked into the kitchen, and Granny opened the back door, it finally came to me. Bamo-slamo, like a bolt of lightning. I needed to make myself sneeze.

"Pablo, grab that lint ball and rub it on my nose," I said to him.

"No, dude. That's weird, and definitely not fun."

I picked up a ball of dryer lint from the floor and rubbed it across my nose. It tickled. I thought I felt a little sneeze coming on, but then it went away. I needed to make my nose itch with a capital *I*.

"Daniel!" Lola called out. She was heading to the laundry room now. "Where are you? I brought you some eucalyptus oil to lubricate your sinuses."

Eucalyptus oil. Oh yeah, that's my grandma all right. Nothing regular like a cherry cough drop for her. She only uses what the natives in New Guinea use.

I rubbed my nose with the lint ball faster this time. I felt it starting to twitch. Come on, sneeze.

"Ah . . . Ah . . . Ah . . . !" Nothing. I was sneezeless.

Then I remembered something I had read in my

favorite book, *The Weird Weird Book of Weird World Records*. I was reading about a woman who set the world record for sneezing (she sneezed for 978 days in a row), and it said that it's a known scientific fact that some people sneeze if they look at a bright light. Hey, it was worth a try.

I looked at the laundry room light. I mean I stared at it really hard. And then, magic happened.

"Ah . . . ah . . . ah . . . ah . . . choooooooo!"

I tell you, science is great. And so is *The Weird Weird Book of Weird World Records*.

CHAPTER 12

The Funkster's Funky Fact #12: The tallest tree in the world is the Australian eucalyptus tree, which can grow as tall as a thirty-eight-story building.

Yup, the sneeze worked. I shot up like a magic bean stalk just as Lola came into the laundry room. My head was still spinning some, so I leaned on the washing machine for balance.

"There you are, dear," said Lola. "What are you doing in the laundry room?"

"Uh . . . reading."

Okay, so it was a lame answer. You try coming up with something after you've just sprouted up from the size of a toe.

"Reading what?" she asked, giving me a funny look.

"I asked him to read the instructions on the washing machine," a voice said, coming to my rescue. It was Granny Nanny, who had just come in the back door. She was hiding the bag of carrots behind her to make it seem like she had been there all along.

"Yeah," I said, jumping in to back her up. "You never know when you might want to do a delicate load. It's important to be prepared."

"Well, that's a very productive use of your time, dear," Lola said. "Sounds like you're feeling better."

"Oh, much better," I said. Granny shot me a look. "I mean, a *little* much better. Not *so* much better that I can go back to school or anything."

"In that case, I'd like you to try out this eucalyptus oil," Lola said. "It's used for nasal congestion all over Australia and New Guinea. Four million koala bears can't be wrong."

She left to get a handkerchief to sprinkle with some eucalyptus oil for me to inhale. That didn't sound fun. But I agreed to it because it would get her out of the room so I could check on Pablo. I looked around for him, but he wasn't easy to spot. Finally I found him lying on a dog biscuit by the dryer, his hands under his head. He gave me a casual wave with his foot.

I wondered how many times he had been in a room with me, just watching as I went through my daily life. I felt kind of sad, realizing I had missed all those years with him. If I could just learn how to shrink whenever I wanted, Pablo and I would be able to catch up on a lot of good times. Suddenly I was in a hurry to get Lola out of there and get started.

If you ask me, and I know you didn't, eucalyptus oil is definitely something you don't want up your nostrils. When Lola held that handkerchief to my nose and I breathed in, the smell was so strong I thought my nose was going to go into orbit. Lola actually had the nerve to suggest I take two sniffs, but I told her that one sniff had cleared my sinuses for the rest of the twenty-first century.

I love Lola, but I was glad when she left, so we could get down to serious business. We had a lot of experiments to conduct if we were going to get some answers.

Granny knew Pablo wasn't much of a science guy, so she set him up at the kitchen table with art supplies. She put out thimbles full of paint and tiny brushes she had made out of toothpicks and cat whiskers. And while we experimented with different foods, he painted a portrait of me. When I looked at it under a magnifying glass, I was shocked.

"This is good," I told him. "I mean really, really good."

"Hey, she didn't name me Pablo Picasso for nothing."

LIN OLIVER

Granny explained that Pablo Picasso was a famous artist. When she saw how talented Pablo was, she gave him that name. And his middle name, Diego, was after another artist guy named Diego Rivera who Granny once danced with at a tango festival. Pablo Picasso Diego Funk. He was lucky to have such a cool name. If my mom had named him, he'd probably be Red-Breasted Nuthatch Funk.

I'll bet you're wondering what exact combination of foods we discovered that would make me shrink. It's a natural question to have at this point.

Well, let me tell you this. Granny and I tried everything. Goulash with carrots. Carrots with raisins. Raisins with cereal. Cereal with yogurt. Yogurt with bananas. Bananas with strawberries. Strawberries with cream. Cream with chocolate sauce. I made Granny try that one three times because it was so delicious.

Nothing worked. I remained exactly the same size.

So next, we decided to go weird. Three salty black olives on a shrimp fork. Cherry pie holding my nose. Chili peppers on an ice cube. Melted Swiss cheese on tangerine skin. Sour cream herring on a dog biscuit. We were getting desperate, guys.

When none of those worked, Granny had another idea.

"Maybe it's not about food," she said. "Maybe shrinking is a state of mind."

So we meditated to get my mind into a shrinking kind of mood. Granny had me visualize small things. I closed my eyes and whispered everything small I could think of.

"Baby chihuahuas, belly button lint, mini frosted wheat flakes, nanobots, miniature golf balls."

"Ding!" Pablo said into the PabloPhone. "Sorry, bro. Those are the same size as regular golf balls."

"How do you know?" I asked him.

"Hey, just because I'm little doesn't mean I live in a cave, you know."

What did that mean? Had he ever played miniature golf? Come to think of it . . . my eight-year-old birthday party was a miniature golf party. It was his birthday too. Had he been there? Maybe Granny tucked him into her purse? Or maybe . . .

"Daniel. You're not concentrating," Granny Nanny said. She was right. This wasn't working. My thoughts were running all over the place.

Pablo jiggled the PabloPhone to let me know he had something to say.

"The Pablo has an idea," he said into the straw. "I think I know what's wrong. Maybe you're out of shrinking energy, dude."

"Shrinking energy? Is there such a thing?" I asked him.

"It's like when I'm painting," he said. "Sometimes, I'm on fire. Then suddenly, bamo-slamo! Poof, dude."

"Poof dude, what?"

"Poof, I'm out of steam. As in done. Tank on empty."

"Do you think that's possible?" I asked Granny. "Could I have run out of shrinking energy?"

"It makes sense, if you think about it," Granny said. "The human body needs rest. That's why we sleep."

"Speaking of which, I'm beat," Pablo said. "I think I'm going to have myself a little lie-down. Maybe catch some TV."

"Granny lets you watch TV in the daytime?" I asked. "Before your homework is done?"

And then I realized. Holy macaroni! Pablo didn't have any homework. Never had. And never would. Man oh man, the small life is the good life.

"It's almost three o'clock anyway," Granny said. "We should clean up before you mom gets home. We'll try again tomorrow."

She put her hand next to the kitchen table, and Pablo stepped aboard. Just before they left, he motioned me over to him. I got down close so I could hear what he was saying.

"Don't brood, dude," he said.

"Okeydokey, smokey," I answered.

"I'll be back, Jack," he said.

"Toodles, poodles," I answered.

We both cracked up. Having a brother was fun.

CHAPTER 13

The Funkster's Funky Fact #13: The word "prom" was first used in the 1890s. It's short for promenade, the march of the guests at the beginning of a formal party.

It was hard to take part in the dinner conversation that night. Not that dinner is ever easy at my house. All Lark does is talk about her feelings on everything from leg hair to unicorns. Robin blabs on about who's wearing what cute uniform to which volleyball game. Goldie talks to Princess and gets in trouble for slipping food to her dolls under the table. Lola cooks weird things like Nigerian Peanut Stew. And when I try to bring up normal stuff like how much memory my hard drive has or whether the Dodgers are going to trade their third baseman for two rookie pitchers, everyone just groans. Except my mom, who tries to look interested even though I know she really wants to talk about the hatching habits of the screech owl.

If you ask me, and I know you didn't, Granny Nanny and I are the only halfway normal ones there.

But on that particular Thursday night, after all I had been through that day, it was especially impossible

for me to sit through dinner. If it hadn't been taco
night, I would have blown off dinner altogether. All
the jabber was about the pre- pre-pre-pre-prom party
the next night. Especially about how Goldie and I
weren't welcome.

"I wish I could come," Goldie said. "Mom, make
them let me."

"Goldie, honey. The girls are entitled to be with
their friends," my mom said. "You and Lola and I will
do something special."

"We'll go in the sweat lodge and I'll read to you

LIN OLIVER

from my *Big Book of Zuni Myths*," Lola said.

I thought Goldie was going to burst into tears right then and there.

"Goldie, try to understand," Lark said. "Robin and I have decided that there are three things you have to have done before you can come to this party. It's important to our women's ritual."

"Like what?" Goldie demanded. "I bet I've done them all."

"Okay," Robin said. "Three questions. Number one. Have you already had your thirteenth birthday?"

"No," Goldie answered. I could tell this wasn't going her way.

"And have you slow-danced with a boy yet?" Robin asked.

"Ick. No."

"And have you ever bought lip gloss?"

"No."

"You see," Robin said. "You're just not qualified to be at a pre-pre-pre-pre-prom party. I'm sorry."

I felt really bad for Goldie. She looked heartbroken.

"You don't want to be at their stupid party anyway, champ," I said, giving her a chuck under the chin.

"And while we're at it, Daniel," Robin said, turning to me. "We're hoping that you'll decide to spend the evening in your room. With the door closed."

"What if I want to watch TV?" I asked. I happened to know that there was a two-hour thrill-and-spill special on motorcycle stunts Friday night, and watching that show on the wide screen was my idea of a totally perfect night.

"Not possible," Lark said. "We'll need the TV to watch my live video blog posts on the big screen."

"But if I get hungry, I'm coming into the kitchen to make a snack."

"Sorry, Big D," Robin said. "We've got dibs. We'll be in there having veggie burgers and salad."

"So in other words," I said with considerable attitude, "you guys are taking over the whole house."

"That sucks," I thought I heard a little voice say.

It was Pablo! Where was he? No one else seemed to hear him. That meant that he was really close to me, but where? I looked around the dinner table. Was he hiding in back of the salt shaker? I didn't see him there. Under the place mat? Nope, not there. In the soup bowl? No sign of him.

"Look down, clown," he said.

Here's a tip: If you're ever looking for your miniature brother and you can't find him, check your pocket. I bet he'll be there.

I looked down and held out my T-shirt pocket so I could see in. There he was, grinning up at me. At least, I think he was grinning. I couldn't see his face that clearly.

"How'd you get in there?" I said aloud, forgetting that the others could hear me.

Granny Nanny looked alarmed. Obviously, she didn't know Pablo had stowed away in my pocket either. But in any case, she didn't want me talking to him in front of everyone. She hadn't kept him a secret for eleven years so I could blow it in one night. Luckily, I have such a bad reputation in my family that no one took me seriously anyway.

"You see, Daniel, that's why you have to stay in your room tomorrow night," Robin said. "Because you do strange things like make lame jokes about someone being in your shirt pocket. I don't think Hailey and Jenna and Kimberly would find that funny. Do you, Lark?"

"No, they appreciate a more womanly kind of humor," Lark said.

"Oh, gag me," said the little voice in my pocket.

I jumped up from the table.

"May I be excused?" I said. "I just forgot that I have a lot of homework to make up before tomorrow."

Without waiting for an answer, I took off for my bedroom. When I got there, I slammed the door shut, reached into my pocket, and pulled Pablo out with two fingers. I put him in the palm of my hand and scrunched down real close to him. He was already talking.

"You going to take that, dude?" he said. "They don't run this house."

"How'd you get in my pocket?"

"The Pablo has his ways," he answered. "I've been in there a lot. You just never knew before."

"You ride around with me?"

"Sure. Now listen up, bro. I think we should protest. We have to let the sisters know that party isn't as hot as they think it is."

I liked his thinking. I wasn't happy either about being sent to my room for the night. And I sure didn't like the way they were treating Goldie.

"What do you have in mind?" I asked him.

"Let me sleep on it," he said. "I'll come up with a good idea."

Oh, yeah. I was sure of that. If there was one thing The Pablo had a lot of, it was good ideas.

CHAPTER 14

The Funkster's Funky Fact #14: The least used stall in a public bathroom is the one closest to the door.

I had to go to school the next day. I mean, I could fake being sick one day with my mom, but not two. Even though she takes care of dogs and cats and cockatoos, she's still a doctor, you know.

Vu picked me up at the usual time. Our school, Ocean Avenue Middle School, is about six blocks from my house. To get there we cut through the Venice canals, which is this really funky area of old houses that are built on actual canals with ducks in them and stuff. When you come out of the canal neighborhood, you're on Ocean Avenue, which has an arcade with some cafés and surf shops and beach stores that sell sand-castle-shaped buckets and flip-flops and sunscreen. Vu's parents' Vietnamese restaurant is there too. Our school is on the other side of the arcade, about two blocks from the good old freezing cold Pacific Ocean.

As we walked, Vu told me all about the visit from Ms. Waters's hissing cockroach.

"It was huge, man. And its name was Maurice."

"You're telling me this bug has a name."

"It's her pet, man. She treats it like it's her son or something."

"That's sick," I heard a little voice say.

Pablo! Now he was coming to school with me? I looked down into my shirt pocket. He wasn't there.

"What's up, Dan?" Vu asked when he saw me rummaging around in my pocket. "You forget a special pen or something?"

"Yeah. The green uni-ball with the fine point. I love that pen."

Vu nodded. He's the kind of guy who gets attached to pens himself.

"Backpack, Jack," the voice said.

I slipped my backpack off my shoulder. I could see that the small pouch at the top where I keep tic tacs and jelly beans and snack stuff was unzipped. I looked in. There was Pablo, munching on a lime jelly bean. He flashed me a little wave.

"Everything okay?" Vu asked. "You look . . . I don't know . . . surprised."

"Everything's great," I said. "I'm just still thinking about . . . uh . . . that . . . green uni-ball pen."

"Wow, I didn't know you were so into pens," Vu said. "I'll have to remember that for your birthday."

Oh, great. Now I had two problems. My miniature brother was in my backpack, and my best friend was going to give me a pen for my birthday.

When we got to school, I told Vu I had a stomach-type emergency, and ran off down the hall to the boy's bathroom. It's a known fact that if you tell anyone but your mom that you have a stomach problem, they're not going to ask you any more questions. I mean, really, who wants to know?

I locked myself into the stall farthest from the door and took off my backpack.

"Are you crazy?" I said to Pablo, who had stuck his head out of the zipper pouch. "You can't come to school with me."

"I've done it before. You don't want me to be ignorant, do you?"

"Granny lets you come?"

"Mostly she teaches me at home, but when you're studying something really cool, I can usually talk her into letting me come with you."

"And then what? You stay in the backpack during class?"

"Sure, I can hear. Sometimes I pop my head out to look at the board. Never during math, though. That's nap time for The Pablo."

Someone knocked on the bathroom stall door.

"This is Mr. Klein. You okay in there? I heard you talking to someone."

Yikes. It was my homeroom teacher.

"It's Daniel Funk, Mr. Klein. I'm fine. I was just . . . um . . . practicing a speech. In case I decide to run for class president. Never hurts to be prepared."

"I suggest you go directly to class, Daniel," he said. "The bell is about to ring."

"Will do, Mr. Klein. And thanks."

I flushed the toilet to make it sound like I was really doing business in there.

"What do we have first?" Pablo asked.

"Science. Ms. Waters."

"Excellent. Let's go check out this hissing cockroach," Pablo said. "I'm thinking he might just come in handy."

"What do you mean, exactly?" I asked him.

But as he started to answer, the bell rang and drowned out what he was saying. There was no time to ask him to repeat it. With everything else I had going on in my life, I didn't want to get detention for being late to class.

CHAPTER 15

The Funkster's Funky Fact #15: A cockroach can live for nine days without its head before it starves to death.

"Hello, Daniel," Ms. Waters said, as I came racing into class. "I'm sorry you were ill yesterday. Feeling better, I presume?"

"Much better, thank you."

I slid into my seat next to Vu. I tossed my backpack down on the floor under my desk like I usually do, but then I remembered Pablo. It didn't seem right to toss him under my seat. I picked up my backpack and put it on top of the desk so he could pop up and look around.

"You missed a very special visit from Maurice," Ms. Waters said.

"Yeah, I heard you brought in your bug."

"Oh no, Daniel. Maurice is not simply a bug. He's a *Gromphadorhina portentosa*. A perfect specimen of what is sometimes called the hissing cockroach."

"He sounds awesome."

"He's more than awesome, Daniel. I've had him for a year. He's not only my pet, he's become a good friend to me. I feel we communicate on a very human level."

If you ask me, and I know you didn't, this was the single weirdest thing any human being had ever said to me. I mean, what kind of person is good friends with a cockroach? Ms. Waters, that's who.

If you're wondering what she looks like, I'll tell you. She's got long black hair that goes down to her waist, a long crooked nose, and really big feet in humongous sandals that have an actual tire tread on the bottom of them. And to top it all off, she's a major cockroach fan.

"If you'd like, Daniel, you may take a few minutes to observe Maurice in his habitat," she said.

"Take me, bro," I heard Pablo say.

"Thanks, Ms. Waters. How can I say no to an offer like that?"

I picked up my backpack and walked to the back of the room where Maurice was sitting in a glass tank on the counter.

"Get me out," Pablo said, sticking his head out of the zipper pouch. "I have to see him."

"Okay, but only for a minute," I whispered, looking around to make sure no one was watching. The kids and Ms. Waters were busy setting up to watch a video on leaf-cutter ants.

I took Pablo out of the pouch and put him on the counter next to Maurice's tank. I put myself between the class and him, just in case anyone decided to look.

"Stay low," I whispered.

"Don't have to, dude. I *am* low."

I put my face down next to the tank to take a good look at Maurice myself. He was big, way bigger than your thumb and probably three times as big as Pablo. He had horns sticking out from his head and two really hairy antennae. My mom says all creatures of nature are beautiful. Sorry, Mom, but I have to tell the truth here. Maurice was one ugly bug.

Pablo tapped on the glass, and Maurice looked up from his log. He wiggled his antennae in what seemed to be not such a friendly way. I think he was trying to throw out a "leave me alone" message. But Pablo wasn't receiving that message. Nope. Instead, he jumped in the air, spun around in a circle, and let go a roundhouse kick right in the direction of Maurice's horns.

This move did not sit well with Maurice. He let out a hiss that sounded like steam shooting out of a teapot.

"Oh, so you want to play tough," Pablo said to him. "Fine, take this."

He started throwing fake martial arts moves at Maurice's tank. He lunged forward, sprang back,

and chopped the air with his hands, making a "hiya" sound every now and then.

Maurice definitely didn't appreciate the karate attack. He rammed the side of the tank with his horns and let go another hiss.

"Hey, buddy, why do you want to mess with someone who watches Kung Fu Theatre every Saturday?" Pablo said, putting his face right next to the glass.

"What are you doing?" I whispered.

"Just checking to see if he's aggressive enough."

"For what?"

"To come to the party, dude! If we invite him, we want to be sure he gives Jenna and Hailey and Kimberly a real show."

"Are you thinking . . ."

"Exactly," Pablo said, without waiting for me to answer. "I think Maurice should attend his first pre-pre-pre-pre-prom party. He'd be a real hit with the girls."

"You mean the women," I said.

Pablo started to laugh like a wild man. And I did too. I saw where he was going, and I liked it a whole lot.

CHAPTER 16

The Funkster's Funky Fact #16: Storing bananas in the refrigerator will make them turn brown or black.

It wasn't easy to talk Ms. Waters into letting me take Maurice home for the weekend. I had to do some really fast thinking.

"Ms. Waters, I have suddenly discovered that I'm totally fascinated with cockroaches," I told her after class. "And I would love the opportunity to study Maurice up close."

"Well, Daniel, he does on occasion spend the night at a student's house," she said. "And he has always enjoyed himself."

I wondered what exactly a cockroach does to enjoy himself. I had this mental picture of Maurice having a spaghetti dinner and then kicking back to watch some wrestling on the wide screen.

"I'd take very good care of him," I told her, "and have him back to you first thing Monday morning. Please, Ms. Waters. This might allow me to grow up and become the next science-type cockroach guy."

"Actually, I do have plans with friends this weekend, so it could work out."

"Make it work out, Ms. Waters. Please. For the future of science and insects and stuff."

That did it. She told me to come to her room after school and she'd put together some things Maurice would need for the weekend.

When Pablo and I went to the science room after school, Ms. Waters had everything ready to go. She handed me a bag containing a rotten peach, a brown banana (news flash—cockroaches like rotten fruit), the top for his tank so he couldn't crawl out, and a plastic baggy of rat chow mix. Yummy. And a little blue blanket she put in his tank at night.

I still wasn't totally clear how we were going to get Maurice to the party, but Pablo was full of plans and jabbered about them all the way home. I couldn't hear much of what he said. It was like having a little chipmunk chattering away in my backpack. But every now and then I'd catch a word or two he was saying like "scream" or "scare" or "laugh my pants off."

When I got home, Robin was in the living room straightening up the house for the party, and Lark was recording it all on her Web cam. Why anyone would want to watch a video of my sister sweeping dust balls off the floor is a total mystery to me.

"Hello, Daniel. Good-bye, Daniel," Robin said without looking up.

"Do you have any feelings about tonight, Daniel?" Lark asked, turning the Web cam on me.

"Depends. Do you consider nauseous a feeling?"

"Not funny, Daniel."

Personally, I thought it was extremely funny. "Okay, here's the truth," I said. "I'm feeling like you're in my space."

"Here we see the male of the species protecting his territory," Lark commented, turning the camera around to shoot herself saying that. As if anyone cared.

I hurried right past her and into my room. I put Maurice's tank down next to the other pets in the Creature Condo Corner. Cutie-Pie, the Siamese fighting fish, gave him a nasty stare-down through the side of her bowl. She looked like she wanted to gobble him up for dinner.

"No, no, Cutie-Pie," I said. "Maurice is our guest, and besides, he has very important work to do tonight."

I opened my backpack and lifted Pablo out.

"It's about time, dude," he said. "I was about to hurl from all that bouncing around in there."

There was a knock on the door.

"GUP alert," Pablo whispered, and darted behind Cutie Pie's bowl.

It was just Granny Nanny.

"How'd it go today, hotshot?" she asked.

"Granny, did you know that Pablo came to school with me?"

"Sure. Who do you think put him in your backpack?"

"Exactly how many times have you let him come to school with me before? Just out of curiosity."

"Let's see now. It started last year when he snuck into your backpack without telling me," she said. "I was worried sick. Thought he'd been eaten by the dog. But when he got home, he was all excited because he had learned so much about the ancient Egyptians."

"I can even write 'bird' in hieroglyphics, dude," Pablo said. "Want to see?"

"Later, gator."

"It didn't seem right to keep him home when he had learned so much," Granny went on. "So this year I send him with you every now and then, especially if you're studying something interesting."

"Like hissing cockroaches," Pablo said.

"Is that what you learned about today?" Granny asked him.

"Oh, big time," Pablo said. "They're very useful creatures. Isn't that right, bro?"

I smiled. It was pretty great having Maurice be our secret.

"How about you, Daniel?" Granny said. "Did you do any shrinking today?"

"Nope. I was just regular-size me."

"That's a good thing, right?" she asked.

I thought about her question for a long time. It was definitely easier to be normal size than to be constantly worried about shrinking, especially since I didn't understand when I would shrink or what made it happen. On the other hand, being little was fun. I thought of what a cool time Pablo and I had diving in the dog dish and sliding down straws and skiing on Detergent Mountain.

Granny was waiting for an answer. I looked at Pablo. He didn't say a word.

"Actually, Granny, I was thinking I'd like to have another shot at shrinking," I said.

Pablo jumped up and down and pumped his fist.

"That's my bro," he said. "Three cheers for The Daniel."

I held up my hand and he high-fived my pinkie finger. There it was again, that butterfly wing sensation.

"There's some fresh goulash in the refrigerator," Granny said. "Let me know if you feel like giving it a whirl. And Pablo, I left a piece of popcorn for your snack. Live it up, boys."

She left, and Pablo and I sat down to make a plan. I got out the PabloPhone and put it up to my ear. We had a lot to discuss, and I didn't want to miss anything.

"What's your idea exactly?" I asked him.

"Simple, dude," he said, putting the green straw tube to his mouth. "When the girls are having dinner, we sneak into Robin's room with my guy Maurice here. After dinner, they come in and we let him go."

"It's a known fact that girls are scared of cockroaches," I added.

"Agreed," Pablo said. "Maurice will hiss like crazy

and just be his general ugly self. They'll scream and run away. And poof, dude. We get to laugh our pants off."

It was perfect. Only one question still had to be answered. Did I want to be big or should I try to shrink for the occasion and watch the fun with my own two little tiny eyes? It was safer to stay big, but more fun to get small.

Hmmm . . . decisions, decisions.

CHAPTER 17

The Funkster's Funky Fact #17: High-heeled shoes were first invented for horseback riding, to keep the rider's feet from slipping forward in the stirrups.

Fun won. I decided to go small.

Let's be honest. It was too good an opportunity to pass up. I mean, just to be in the front row, so to speak, when Robin and her pals started screaming and yelling in full-out panic mode—well, it was the chance of a lifetime.

In case you're thinking I'm a real jerk, let me admit this right now. I know releasing Maurice at the party wasn't the nicest thing in the world to do. But I felt I was teaching Robin and Lark a lesson about kicking me out and acting like I didn't even live there. And for treating Goldie that way too. Someone had to stand up for her rights.

Robin's party was starting at seven, so at six o'clock I sat myself down in the kitchen with a big bowl of Granny's goulash. I ate until I thought my stomach was going to explode. Luckily, a few giccups made my stomach feel better. Then, just to give my shrinking powers an extra oomph, I closed my eyes and thought small thoughts. I should have waited to

do that until after I finished the goulash, because I dribbled a lot of gravy down the front of my shirt.

Here's a tip: Eat with your eyes open, guys. It gives the food a much better shot at reaching your mouth.

Mom and Lola and Goldie passed by, heading out to the sweat lodge for an evening of Zuni fun and games. Mom was carrying Samantha the Womanly Cat. Robin had made it very clear that cats with eye patches were definitely NOT allowed at her party.

Poor Goldie, she looked miserable. To cheer her up, Mom had let her wear a pair of her high-heeled shoes. But Goldie knew that was lame. I mean, she wanted to be strutting with the girls, not doing native dances around a pile of hot rocks.

As I finished the goulash, Granny Nanny put a little silver bell on the table.

"Ring this if you start to feel anything," she said. "I'll come right away."

"Why don't you just stay with me, Granny?"

"I had an inspiration this afternoon," she said, "and when the artistic spirit strikes, you have to go with it."

"What kind of inspiration?"

"I'm building a new house for Pablo from a hollowed-out golf ball. It's going to look like a space station from the future. And if he straps himself in, he can roll while he sleeps. The whole idea came to me in a dream."

"That sounds so cool, Granny. Pablo will love it."

"Well, concentrate, hotshot. Maybe you can spend the night in there sometime too."

She left and I started concentrating like crazy. I

LIN OLIVER

thought small thoughts. But nothing happened.

At a few minutes before seven, Robin came into the kitchen.

"Hello, Daniel. Good-bye, Daniel," she said. That seemed to be the only thing she could say that day.

"Fine, I'm going," I said. "Have fun with your veggie burgers."

As I went back to my room, I heard the doorbell ring. I peeked out the window and saw Hailey, Jenna, and Kimberly standing on our front porch. They were in fancy dresses like they were going to a prom. If you ask me, and I know you didn't, I cannot see the point of getting all decked out to come over and shove in a few pathetic veggie burgers.

Pablo was waiting for me in my room. I had left him in charge of watching Maurice.

"How's the cockroach-sitting?" I asked, crouching down next to the Critter Condos so I could hear his answer.

"I've got him all fired up, bro," he said. "The dude definitely does not like the martial arts. Hey, I notice you're not small."

"I tried. I ate a ton of goulash, but no luck so far. Meanwhile, we have to get busy. The party's starting."

"Let the games begin," Pablo said.

I got an old shoe box and poked air holes in the top. I tried to transfer Maurice in there, but he wouldn't come into my hand. So I took a chunk of his rotten banana, smeared it on my finger and held it out to him. Man, old Maurice practically pole-vaulted into my hand. He was a real fan of the rotten banana. I put him in the shoe box and closed the lid.

I could hear that the girls were winding up dinner, so I picked up Pablo and we tiptoed down to Robin's room. She had put out a card table with hand mirrors, lip glosses, brushes and combs, and bottles of hair goop. The bottles were all called things like Strawberry Patch Extra Hold and Peachy Mousse and Plum Super Shine. There was even a Banana Bonanza, whatever that was. The whole table was like a fruit salad for your hair.

"I've got my hiding place all picked out," Pablo said. "The old Barbie house over on that shelf."

"That's not a Barbie house," I said. "That's Miss Ginny's Jazzy Power Gym."

"I don't like that you know this, dude."

"Are you kidding? Tracking down Miss Ginny was a huge deal. Robin had to have a volleyball doll, and it's not easy to find a jock doll with a jock house. Mom looked all over the Internet until Miss Ginny and her Jazzy Power Gym saved the day."

LIN OLIVER

"Well good," Pablo said, "because I'm going to make myself at home in her fine set-up."

I put him down and he found a hiding place behind a row of Miss Ginny's Jazzy Lockers. I had planned to hide with him to watch the fun, but I still hadn't shrunk. I wondered if maybe my shrinking days were over.

I could hear the girls coming down the hall. How could you miss them? They were all talking at once about hair and lips and shoes and mascara and boys and deejays and—oh, did I mention hair? Yeah, there was a lot of hair talk going on.

I had to decide quickly what to do. I couldn't let them find me there holding a cockroach. And I really didn't want to go back to my room and miss the action. This had suddenly gotten very complicated.

Then I saw it. In the closet. Robin's old toy chest.

It was pretty big, and if I curled up in a ball, I thought I could fit in. I ran over and threw the lid open. Inside were all of Robin's old stuffed animals— Mr. Teddy and Mrs. Kitty and Miss Snuggles and Mr. Lion and Mrs. Tiger. (Don't ask. Robin must have had something against first names.)

The girls were right outside the door, and I didn't have a second to waste. I jumped in the toy chest and pulled the lid down over my head just as they came in. I was too big and the lid didn't shut totally. There

was a small crack left open, so I took Mr. Teddy and put him in front of my face. You'd have to look real carefully to see my eyes and the top of my head. If I hid behind Mr. Teddy and stayed very still, I didn't think they'd notice me.

The girls gathered around the table, attacking those bottles of hair stuff like they were Snickers bars.

"Doesn't the Peachy Mousse smell dreamy?" Jenna said. Or maybe that was Kimberly.

"Do you guys think my bangs look cute like this?" Hailey asked.

"They're the cutest," Robin answered. "Let's add some mousse, for volume."

From my spot in the toy chest, I could see Pablo peeking out from Miss Ginny's locker room. He caught my eye and signaled something to me. I couldn't see exactly what he was doing, but I figured he was telling me to open the shoe box and let Maurice out.

Why not? Now was as good a time as any. Besides, I didn't think I could take another second of mousse talk.

I slid the lid off the shoe box. Maurice scurried out through the open crack in the toy chest and headed straight to the table where the girls were gathered. He ran up the table leg and climbed on those bottles like they were his own personal jungle gym. He must have smelled their fruity scents. I mean, one was called Banana Bonanza. Man, that bug was in cockroach heaven!

When the girls saw him, they freaked out big-time. And I mean BIG-TIME.

"Eeuuwwwwwww! A bug!" Hailey screamed. "Eeuuwwwwwww!"

"I hate bugs!" Jenna shrieked. "Get me out of here!"

"A cockroach!" Kimberly screeched. "They're filthy!"

You wouldn't have believed the yelling and hollering and squealing that came out of their mouths. A guy could lose his hearing.

Robin jumped up and started chasing Maurice, trying to get him off the table. But his fruit-loving nose (if cockroaches have noses, that is, which I seriously doubt) was telling him to stay.

"Why are we women afraid of bugs?" Lark said, turning the Web cam on herself. "Is it part of our nature or have we learned fear?" (If you want the answer, check her blog at I'mSoBoring.com. But if you ask me, and I know you didn't, I'd *definitely* skip it.)

I moved Mr. Teddy aside so I could catch a glimpse of Pablo. He was laughing his pants off. I'm not proud of it, but I was having the time of my life myself. The girls' reaction was even better than I thought it would be. They ran screaming out of the room and down the hall and out onto the front porch. Then they just stood there and continued to scream. I knew that if Vu heard them, he'd tell Spencer who'd tell Nicky who'd tell his sister Emily, and then everyone at Ocean Avenue Middle School would know what happened at Robin's party. The thought tickled me so much I let out a little laugh.

And that's when it happened. The growling in my

LIN OLIVER

eyeballs. The bubbling in my nose. The buzzing in my fingers. The whistling in my knees.

Bamo-slamo, before you knew it I was—you guessed it—the size of the fourth toe on my left foot. I was looking straight into the face of Mr. Teddy, who was suddenly a huge brown grizzly bear towering over tiny little me.

What had made me shrink? I was sure it had something to do with the goulash. But why at that moment? Was it the darkness? Or that I was laughing really hard? Was it the noise level in the room? Or was it something I thought about? Or did I just have a burst of shrinking energy, if such a thing even exists.

I was going to have to figure this out.

But not then. No, then was *definitely* not the moment. And here's why.

Robin.

Now, it's a known fact in the Funk family that my sister Robin has a temper. So I should have thought about the possibility that she'd lose it, which she did at that moment in a major way. She came running back from the front porch in a one-of-a-kind Robin Funk temper tantrum.

"Where are you, you stupid bug?" she screamed. "You're going to have to face me."

And then she pulled off her sparkly high-heeled shoe and started running around the room looking for him.

"I'm going to squash you," she hollered. "Who do you think you are, coming here without an invitation! You're a goner, Mister!"

Maurice had just been hanging out on the table, trying to get a taste of the Banana Bonanza. But when Robin came after him with her shoe, he took off like an Olympic sprinter. He ran down the table leg and scooted across the floor really fast. She followed him, slapping at him with her shoe.

"You scared my new friends, you stupid bug. That's a big no-no."

With each word, she pounded the floor with her shoe. She kept missing him, but Robin was a jock, and I knew that sooner or later she'd get him.

This was not good. Let's be honest. This was terrible.

My sister was trying to kill Maurice. Ms. Water's good friend! Who she communicates with on a human level. Who I had promised to return safely on Monday morning. How could I ever tell Ms. Waters that I had let her good friend get . . . get . . . get . . . squished by a prom shoe?

CHAPTER 18

The Funkster's Funky Fact #18:
The first teddy bear appeared in 1902 and was
named after President Theodore Roosevelt.

I couldn't save Maurice. I couldn't even climb out of the toy chest. But I had to try. He was in real danger. Trust me. You wouldn't want to be on the other end of Robin's shoe when she's having a hissy fit.

If I could just get to the top of the toy chest, I could jump down. I tried scaling Mr. Teddy's face. It wasn't hard to pull myself up by his fur, and I made good progress until I reached his snout. But then, I accidentally stepped on his slippery plastic nose, lost my footing, and fell all the way down to his paw.

"It's over for you," Robin was shouting to Maurice. Then I heard the *slap, slap, slap* of her shoe.

"Hang in there, Maurice," a tiny voice called out. "I'm coming!"

It was Pablo! He said something more, but his voice was so little and far away that I couldn't make out his words. I could tell he was out of Miss Ginny's Jazzy Power Gym, and I wondered how he had done it. I knew the locker room had a miniature whirlpool and showers. And the main workout room had teensy treadmills and a trampoline. Maybe he had bounced on the trampoline and somersaulted out of the gym and onto the floor. That was definitely possible. I'd seen him do a jackknife, and that boy could get some serious air.

"Slow down, you little beast," Robin was yelling at Maurice. "You're toast!"

I had to try harder to get out of the chest. Robin was on fire, and Pablo was going to need my help.

Mrs. Tiger, who was perched on top of Miss Snuggles, was closest to the top. I figured if I could get to her ear, I could at least make it to the top to see out. So I started climbing. Her fur wasn't as long or as soft as Mr. Teddy's and it was tough going. This time I was careful to avoid the plastic nose problem. I did brush against her whiskers, though, and they tickled me under the armpit. I couldn't help laughing. Sorry, Maurice. I didn't mean to laugh when your life was at stake, but I have extremely ticklish armpits.

The shoe-thumping continued outside, which was a good sign. Maurice was still in the game. When I made it to Mrs. Tiger's ear, I pulled myself across a black stripe and a yellow stripe and looked out.

What I saw was amazing.

Pablo was in Miss Ginny's Jazzy Gym Jeep, driving

across the floor of Robin's room. Can you believe him? He never even mentioned that he knew how to drive! Anyway, he was driving in big circles around Maurice, trying to herd him closer and closer to the bed. Robin was chasing the Jazzy Jeep now, slapping at it with her high-heeled shoe.

"Stupid remote control car," she was screaming. "Where's your off button, anyway?"

Okay, I can buy that she thought maybe she had stepped on the remote and activated Miss Ginny's Jazzy Gym Jeep. But who did she think Pablo was? Earth to Robin's brain . . . anyone home?

"Stupid action figure," she yelled. "Stupid Daniel's stupid toy."

Okay. There was my answer.

When you think about it, Robin wasn't entirely crazy to think Pablo was an action figure. I mean, he does wear action figure clothes and he did have this stiff look plastered on his face. I could see how she came up with that thought. Besides, most people don't go around thinking that a toe-sized mini person is driving a toy car around their room. You have to admit, it wouldn't be your first thought, either.

Pablo was a good driver, good enough to avoid getting crushed by my crazed sister and her evil shoe. It was Maurice I was worried about. He was running all around, hissing like a snake, and looking frightened and mean at the same time. As I watched him, I realized how big he was, compared to Pablo. He could eat him alive! Maybe it was Pablo I should be worried about.

My mind was racing. I knew Maurice was in danger from The Shoe. And I somehow felt Pablo was in danger from Maurice. And me, I was stuck in the toy chest.

It was time to bring on the sneeze.

"Okay, Mrs. Tiger," I said. "Do your thing."

I put my face down on the tip of her ear and rubbed my nose along the fur. It wasn't furry enough to make my nose really itch. It needed to itch with a capital *I*, and the ear fur just wasn't cutting it. I needed something that tickled.

The whiskers!

I leaped off Mrs. Tiger's ear and landed on her nose. I don't want to brag, but I have to say I totally nailed the landing. But this was no time for gymnastics.

I grabbed hold of two whiskers and brought them to my face, rubbing them across the tip of my nose. It started to itch. I kept rubbing the whiskers until finally, finally . . .

"Ah . . . ah . . . ah . . . chooooooooo!"

And before you could say Miss Ginny's Jazzy Gym

Jeep, I had popped back up to my normal size.

"Oowwww," I yelled, because I had totally slammed my head on the lid of the toy chest.

Robin whirled around and stared at me.

"When did you get here?" she said. "And what are you doing with Mrs. Tiger? Put her down! She's very special to me."

As I looked down on the floor, I saw Maurice scoot under Robin's bed, with Pablo in the jeep right behind him.

"I heard the screaming," I said. "Seems like you have a little bug problem."

"Eeuuuww! He just ran under the bed," Robin said. "That's so totally creepy."

I took the shoe box from the toy chest and hurried over to the bed. I got down on my hands and knees and looked under it. Miss Ginny's Jazzy Gym Jeep was there, but Pablo wasn't in it. Maurice was running in circles around the car. I wondered where Pablo was.

"Here, Mr. Buggy," I said, crawling all the way under the bed and holding out my hand. I knew my fingers still smelled like rotten banana, and I think we all know how Maurice feels about rotten bananas. Sure enough, he hopped into my hand like we were old pals. Slowly I took him from under the bed, set him down in the shoe box, and put the cover on.

You're not going to believe this, but Robin actually threw her arms around me and gave me a hug.

"Daniel, that was so cool," she said. "How did you do that?"

"Us guys just have a way with bugs, I guess."

"I'll go tell the girls it's safe." But before she left, she turned and said something Robin doesn't say often. "How can I thank you, Daniel?"

"For starters, next time you have a party, you can invite Goldie. She can talk about cute bangs just as well as your other friends."

"How do you know what we talked about?" Robin asked, giving me a suspicious look.

Oops.

Here's a tip: When you've almost let the secret out that you happen to be able to shrink and eavesdrop on your sister's party, you should change the subject really fast.

"Lucky guess. And by the way," I said, changing the subject really fast, "maybe you should point out that it's not so terrible to have a guy around the house. We have rights too, you know."

"I'm going to tell them right now," Robin said. "You'll be a hero." She ran out of the room just as my mom was coming in.

"What is going on here?" she asked. "I thought I heard screaming."

"You just noticed? Wow, nice hearing, Mom."

"We were chanting in the sweat lodge, honey, and it's hard to hear anything else. You should come join us."

"Can't. I have to take care of him." I slid the top of the shoebox off just enough so she could get a look at Maurice.

"Oh, what a handsome *Gromphadorhina portentosa*,"

she said. "Look how fat he is around the middle. He must have just eaten a big meal."

I didn't like the sound of that. I mean, I had been with Maurice for the last couple of hours, and he hadn't eaten anything. The only time I hadn't been with him was when he was under the bed . . . with Pablo. And where was Pablo, anyway? The question had been bothering me.

"Hey, Mom," I said casually. "A cockroach like this, he couldn't eat something the size of like . . . say . . . the fourth toe on my foot, could he?"

"Daniel, you are such a funny boy," she laughed. "Who ever heard of such a question?"

"I mean it, Mom."

She gave me a really odd look. But my mom has always told us that she would answer any question we had about anything as honestly as she could. So she did.

"Cockroaches are scavengers," she said, "which means they will eat almost anything. They can chew. So I guess they could eat something the size of a toe, in theory anyway. Why do you ask, honey?"

I couldn't answer. I couldn't even look at her. I felt my heart starting to beat fast.

"We'll look it up tomorrow, if you're still interested," she said as she left.

The second she was out of the room, I dropped down on my hands and knees and crawled under Robin's bed. The jeep was still there, but no Pablo. I ran to my room and got a flashlight. I came back and searched under the bed, shining the flashlight into every corner. No Pablo. I called his name, over and over. No Pablo.

I took the top off the shoe box and stared at Maurice. He did look fatter around the middle. And he was sound asleep. I remember reading that after a snake swallows his prey, he sleeps while he's digesting it.

I was dizzy, and there was a lump in my throat, like the kind you get just before you cry.

"Pablo," I called. "Where are you?"

But there was no answer.

CHAPTER 19

The Funkster's Funky Fact #19:
There are 336 dimples on a golf ball.

I crumbled to the floor in a heap. I couldn't stand. I couldn't walk. I couldn't think. Pablo had been eaten by Maurice as he was trying to save Maurice's life. Pablo was the real hero.

All my life I had wanted a brother. And finally I had one. And not just any brother, the perfect brother.

Now he was gone. It was too sad for words.

"Oh, Pablo," I said out loud. "I love you, dude. I really love you."

"Hey, right back at you," said a little voice.

I looked down on the floor, and there he was. Soaking wet, with nothing on but a baggy pair of Batman boxer shorts.

"Pablo, I thought Maurice had eaten you."

"Dude, you think I'd let that bug get me?" He did a roundhouse kick and a karate chop in the air, almost losing his boxers. "No way, bro. The Pablo has moves."

"But the jeep . . . it was under the bed."

"Hey, when you get a parking space like that, it pays to leave the car and walk."

"Where were you?"

"In the whirlpool, dude. Miss Ginny's Jazzy Whirlpool is totally awesome."

"But I was calling you."

"Sorry. Hard to hear when the whirlpool is fired up. No biggie, though."

"No biggie? Pablo, I thought I had lost you," I said.

"You and Granny, bro. Always worrying."

I scooped him up in my hand and hugged him between my palm and my chest.

"Ease up, dude. I'm feeling the love and all, but you're crushing me."

I let him go. But I can tell you this, I sure didn't want to.

I begged Granny Nanny to let him sleep in my room that night. His new golf ball house was finished, and it was the coolest thing you ever saw. It looked like a white-domed spaceship with dimples all over the top. Granny hadn't quite worked out how to make it safe for sleeping while it was rolling. But that was okay. We put it on a sock so it would stay put all night. I didn't want to take the chance of Pablo rolling away. After all, the world's a dangerous place when you're the size of a toe.

As I settled into bed that night, my mind was full

of questions about our future, Pablo's and mine. Would I ever really find out what made me shrink? Would he ever grow? Would we always be together? Boy, I hoped so.

I closed my eyes and curled up on my side, which is my ace sleeping position. Just as I got comfortable, I felt something poking me in the arm, then in the back. I rolled over and saw the long green straw of the PabloPhone coming out of the golf ball house and poking around like an antenna on a snail. I took the end and held it up to my mouth.

"Pablo?" I whispered into the straw. "Is that you?"

I put the PabloPhone up to my ear.

"It's me, dude," I heard him say. "I've been thinking. What's up in school next week?"

"The usual," I said. "Math, spelling, science, history."

"Can you take a day off?"

"Maybe. It's a tough week, though. I have a project due on Egyptian mummies."

It was quiet for a minute. Then I heard him say . . .

"Maybe I'll come."

"To school?" I asked. "Why would you come to school with me when you could hang around here and do whatever you want?"

"The Pablo would be a great mummy," he said.

"Wrap me up and turn me loose. I tell you, bro, I see some serious fun in our future."

I had no idea what exactly Pablo was thinking, but it was already sounding pretty wild. Man oh man, I thought to myself. This having a brother thing was just totally great. I mean really. *Wrap me up and turn me loose!* Whatever that was about had to be fun.

"Hey, Pablo, can I ask you something?" I whispered into the straw.

"Sure. Shoot, bro."

"Who's older, you or me?"

"Me, dude. I was in your ear, remember? Which means *all* of me was born before *all* of you."

"So does that make you the big brother?"

"You better believe it, dude. The Pablo rules."

I flicked off the light and curled back up into my favorite position. As I closed my eyes and fell asleep, I could feel myself smile when I thought how lucky I was to have my little big brother sleeping next to me.

CHAPTER 20

The Funkster's Funky Fact #20: The first magnifying glasses were called "flea glasses" because they were used to look at fleas and other tiny insects.

Pablo thinks that because he's the "big brother" he should have the last word. So here it is. You might need a magnifying glass to read it. No surprise there. I mean, what do you expect when the guy writing it is the size of a toe?

Yo, dudes.
It's The Pablo saying
Got to jet, Brett...
BUT
I'll be back, Jack.
Later gator,
The Pablo